MAGIC IN FAIRYLAND

MAGIC IN FAIRYLAND

Marjorie Holstead

Illustrations by
Michael Avery

The Book Guild Ltd
Sussex, England

The Book Guild Ltd
25 High Street
Lewes, Sussex

First published 1996
© Marjorie Holstead 1996
Set in Souvenir Light
Typesetting by Southern Reproductions (Sussex)
Crowborough, Sussex
Printed in Great Britain by
Antony Rowe Ltd
Chippenham, Wiltshire.

A catalogue record for this book is
available from the British Library

ISBN 1 85776 058 1

CONTENTS

To Karen, Pamela, Andrea and David

THE FAIRY TOOTH

Fairy Marigold had toothache! Whoever heard of a fairy having toothache! All the other fairies stared at her in astonishment – and even the Fairy Queen was surprised. 'We've never needed a dentist in Fairyland,' she said. 'I wonder what we must do?'
Fairy Marigold sat on a mushroom feeling very glum indeed. It was bad enough having toothache, but fancy, no-one knew what to do!

After a long think the Queen said, 'I know, you'd better go to the clever Wizard. He'll probably tell you what to do.'

So the little fairy started on her way. The Wizard lived on top of a hill, and she had to fly high above the treetops for a very long time. At last she saw his gorgeous palace gleaming and twinkling in the rays of the sun. She knocked on the enormous front door and straight away it was opened by a little elf dressed in green velvet.

'Why, hello Fairy Marigold,' he said. 'You do look weary today; what's the matter?'

'I have toothache,' sighed Marigold.

'Toothache?' echoed Nimble (for that was his name).

'Now don't you start,' said the fairy, 'and why on earth shouldn't a fairy have toothache?'

'All right, all right,' hastily added the little elf, 'don't get ruffled!'

'Please may I see the Wizard?' begged Marigold.

'Of course. Come this way,' and he opened wider the door.

Sprightly the elf led the way up a winding staircase where, at the top, gazing out of the window, the Wizard reclined on a lovely red velvet couch..

'I expect you've come here to have your toothache cured,' he announced.

'How did you guess?' gasped the fairy.

'Aha, that is part of my magic,' murmured the old Wizard.

'No-one in Fairyland knew what to do,' complained Marigold.

'Well, you've come to the right person now,' he said, with a smile. 'Does it hurt an awful lot?'

'Oh, yes! And it's been going on for simply ages.' The little fairy gingerly touched her sore cheek.

'Do you know what my beautiful palace is made of?' asked the Wizard suddenly.

'I have never thought about it,' she replied.

'Well, my little elves are very busy, you know. They go, every single night, into Humanland and bring back ivory. I'm thinking of building another extension on to this palace. We really need another ballroom, so that we can invite all you fairies when it comes to my birthday.

'All human children put their first teeth under their pillows or under carpets for us to collect. We can't just take the ivory and not give them anything in return, so we leave a sixpence for each tooth. We couldn't think what to give them, till one of my elves saw a child buying an icecream with a little round silver object. He tells me they don't always call it "sixpence" now, and maybe soon we will have to make a larger coin called "5p". However, that is in the future. One day my messenger was lucky enough to find a lost sixpence in the gutter. I copied the design (such a simple matter with my superb wizardry!) and the workshop elves make them for me out of the silver we mine from the mountain.'

'That's very interesting, but I can't see what this has to do with my toothache,' grumbled Fairy Marigold.

'Patience! All in good time,' frowned Wizard Winkle. 'Now I come to your part in all this. Your toothache will not go until you bring back a tooth belonging to a little girl called Marigold – like yourself.'

'Good gracious! And where do I find her?' exclaimed the fairy.

'That I don't know.' The Wizard turned to Nimble and told him to bring a silver sixpence from the store in the cellar. He was back very soon, puffing and blowing with the weight of the shiny silver coin which he had reverently placed on a velvety pansy petal in the centre of a bark tray.

Fairy Marigold thanked Wizard Winkle for his advice and the sixpence. The latter she tucked in a cobweb haversack, and flew away quickly, determined to find the little girl Marigold, wherever she happened to be.

It was growing dusk now, and all the woodland creatures were busily preparing for bed.

'Where are you off to this late hour?' they enquired.

'Do you know a little girl called Marigold?' begged the fairy.

'I know a sweet child called Mary Rose,' ventured a

rabbit. 'She picks bluebells and primroses in this very wood.'

'No, that's not the one,' and on she flew through the forest, till she came to a cluster of houses. 'Now, I wonder if any small girls live here,' she murmured.

So, she peeped in at the bedroom windows wherever the curtains were a little open and, at first, she was so unlucky – all the children were boys!. She was also wondering how in the world she would find out the name of the little girl if she did come across one!

She rested on a windowsill feeling very forlorn, and from a nest above a little sparrow popped up his head and twittered, 'What have we here? A fairy sitting on the windowsill! You'll catch cold, my dear.'

'Well, that's nothing compared with my toothache,' moaned Fairy Marigold. 'I have to find a child called Marigold, and when I take away her tooth from under the pillow, my toothache will go. Do you know anyone by that name, Mr Sparrow?'

'Fancy that. I know the very little girl you want, but she lives on a farm away from the village.'

'Oh, thank you, thank you,' she shouted, and flew as fast as she could to a whitewashed farm in the midst of the fields. Sure enough, as she peeked through the window, there was the sweetest little girl with golden hair and lovely pink cheeks. She was fast asleep, and smiling as if she knew that a shining new sixpence would be hers on the morrow.

Now, how was Fairy Marigold to get in? All the doors were closed, and the bedroom window too.

'That's a problem,' muttered Marigold. 'Ah, but what about the chimney?'

She slid down very carefully, trying not to dirty her lovely rainbow wings. Fortunately it was a long time

11

since a fire had been lit, for it was nearly summer. She hopped onto the hearth and looked around.

Aha, a nice floral rug. Diligently she searched, but no, the tooth certainly wasn't under it. She was quite out of puff afterwards, and flopped down to consider matters.

'As it isn't under this rug, I'm sure the tooth must be under Marigold's pillow. I'd better sprinkle a little fairy dust over the child to take her deeper into dreamland.'

Gently Fairy Marigold showered some golden dust over the golden curls, and wriggled carefully under the snow-shite pillow. Oh, what joy, the coveted tooth at last! As her fingers felt the smooth ivory, the fairy sighed with relief. Yes, her toothache had magically disappeared.

She dropped a kiss on the child's forehead, and pushed the silver sixpence under the pillow. Then, with a last look at the sleeping Marigold, she flew up the chimney, and away to Fairyland. How pleased they all were to see Fairy Marigold smiling again!

The very next morning she flew to see Wizard Winkle, for she wished to thank him and also to show him the ivory tooth carefully placed in her cobweb haversack.

'Would you like it?' she smiled.

'Dear me, no!' said he. 'You must keep that special one in a safe place or you might have toothache again!'

'I know,' said Marigold, 'I will help your elves to bring in the teeth. I think it's a lovely thing to do.'

And that is why little boys and girls sometimes dream extra special, sweet dreams. For, whenever Fairy Marigold calls, she sprinkles them with fairy dust.

FAIRY ROSEBUD

There was once a little fairy called Rosebud. She wore a beautiful pink dress edged with tiny red rosebuds and a garland of rosebuds on her hair and she carried a silver wand with a ruby star. On her feet were the most delightful silver slippers with ruby buckles. These slippers were very special for, without them, she would not be able to find her way back to Fairyland when she became old enough to visit Humanland. You would think that this little fairy would be quite content to play all day in Fairyland with her little sisters, but no!

One day she decided she would go into the outside world and, when no-one was looking, she flew away. She was entranced with the wonderful things she saw: giant houses, bridges, rivers and deep, dark forests. The busy humans amazed her as they dashed here and there in their cars and buses. All day she flew about and had a lovely time playing with the birds who were very surprised to see such a young fairy out and about.

Towards tea-time she felt a little tired, so she sat down to rest in a lovely meadow. Soon she was fast asleep and did not notice a tiny rabbit pop out of her burrow and stare in surprise at Rosebud.

'What gorgeous slippers!' the rabbit said, and

without any more ado she popped them on her feet. 'I must show Mum,' she chortled, and the little rabbit began to run towards the rabbit-hole.

Just then, Fairy Rosebud woke up and saw to her dismay that her lovely shoes were disappearing. Quickly she ran after the rabbit and caught her up at last in a little round room where her mum and dad were having afternoon tea.

'My slippers!' gasped the fairy. 'I simply must have them or I will not be able to go home.'

'You should not have fallen asleep,' said Mrs Rabbit severely. 'A good thing that it was only our Rowena who stole them. You may have them back, but first you must promise to do something for us.'

The Fairy Rosebud was only too pleased to promise.

Mrs Rabbit wanted her to go and see a naughty dog called Bowzer who was always chasing them and making the whole family very unhappy. 'He lives in Cherry-Tree Lane,' she said.

So off the fairy flew, now wearing her special slippers, for the rabbit family knew that no fairy ever goes back on her promise.

Sure enough, there was Bowzer having a lovely time burying a bone in his back garden.

'Well, fancy seeing such a pretty little fairy out on her own,' he barked.

'Never mind that,' said Rosebud. 'Have you been chasing the rabbit family?'

He hung his head. 'Well, you see, they are the only ones I *can* chase. I'm scared of Ginger, the big dog up the road. It's a change for me to know they're afraid of me!'

The little fairy thought for a minute, then said, 'I know. I'll wave my wand and you'll become brave.

Then you'll no longer run away from the other dogs. But you must promise never to chase the rabbit family again!'

Bowzer stuck his chest out, chased his tail three times, then sped up the road to test out his new courage!

Fairy Rosebud had to hurry because it was getting dark and the gates of Fairyland would be closing soon. With a sigh of relief she flew through the golden gates only to find the Queen waiting for her with a very serious expression on her face.

'Just where have *you* been?' she asked, and the fairy blushed, and told the Queen of her experiences in the outside world.

At last, when Fairy Rosebud had finished, the Queen sighed and said, 'You're lucky you didn't meet with more serious trouble, but I'm glad some good has come out of your disobedience. The rabbit family and Bowzer will be happier. We have all been very worried about you. All the older fairies have been flying all day looking for you and they have not been able to do their usual work. Perhaps you're wiser now and will not go away again until I give you permission.'

'I will be good,' cried Fairy Rosebud, and she did not go out again till she came of age.

Do you know how she spent the next four weeks? Why, making a new dress and rosebud garland, for they were all dirty and tattered from her scramble down the rabbit-hole!

PUDDING THE PIXIE

Andrea, the Fairy Queen, sighed as she picked up her crystal scent bottle. Oh, she did wish she had some new perfume; she was tired of the same fragrance, delightful though it was. She dabbed the glass stopper on her wrists and behind her ears, then wrinkled her nose as she distinctly smelled a quite obnoxious aroma. She took hold of the bottle and breathed deeply. Ugh! The perfume (if you could call it that) was most decidedly 'off'.

'How could that happen?' she murmured. 'The scent was quite all right yesterday.'

What she didn't know, only Sammy Sprite could tell. He had stolen into her room while she was asleep and had poured some green pond water into the bottle. What a naughty sprite he was! He had been banished to Tanglewood for sticking Fiona Fairy's wings together. Now what would happen if he was found out?

Andrea rang her little silver bell and in flew her chief lady-in-waiting, Fairy Maybelle. 'Just look at my perfume bottle! See, the scent has turned a horrid muddy green, and oh, how it smells!'

Fairy Maybelle held her nose. 'I can smell it from here, Fairy Queen!'

'I must have some new perfume,' pouted the

17

Queen, and it must be ready for the ball on Saturday. All my friends will be coming. Whoever heard of a Fairy Queen being without perfume!'

'I'll fly down to the workshop right away,' cried Maybelle. 'The elves must send up a fresh bottle immediately.'

'Wait, wait,' interrupted Queen Andrea. 'I have an idea. I would love some really special new fragrance. I'm tired of the usual flower scents. How about organising a competition? The fairy or pixie who makes up an entirely new and lovely perfume for me shall be given a new toadstool house, and will dance the first dance with me at the ball!'

Fairy Maybelle clapped her hands in glee. 'That should set everyone busy,' she chortled. 'What fun!'

'Go,' commanded Queen Andrea, 'tell our fairy messengers to spread the news throughout Fairyland!'

'At once, Your Majesty,' cried Fairy Maybelle.

Soon all Fairyland was atwitter with the exciting news. Off flew fairies and pixies in all directions, stopping only to don haversacks. 'My secret recipe for Bell Flower Scent cannot fail to win,' boasted Fairy Blossom. 'Now fly away Fairy Thistledown, you can't come and peek!'

'I shall be away from home two nights to find my special ingredients,' solemnly pronounced Percival Pixie.

'That's nothing,' interrupted Jiffy Gnome, 'it will take all week to fly to and from my special flower patch!'

Only Pudding the Pixie sat gloomily outside his mushroom house. Really his home was so small he hadn't room to move about. No wonder! He was as

round as a roly-poly pudding. His face suddenly lit up. He'd make his favourite jam lattice tart. *He* wasn't going to join in the mad scramble to make perfume! What could beat the smell of goodies cooking? He waddled inside, and before long had a strawberry-jam tart inside the oven. Soon a delectable aroma wafted from the mushroom cottage.

Robin Redbreast sniffed the air. 'Oh, goody! Pudding the Pixie is making a treat again!' Soon there would be scrumptious crumbs to eat!

Pudding the Pixie brought out his tart and put it to cool on a little stool outside the green door. 'Hi, Robin Redbreast, come to help me eat some tart?'

'Oh, thank you, Pudding,' chirped Robin, 'but how come you're not out in the lanes searching for special flowers to make the Queen's new scent?'

'What's the use?' sighed Pudding. 'My wings won't take me very far, I'm so fat.'

'You don't need to use them very much,' said Robin. 'I happen to know where a very special flower grows and, if you add its petals to lots of wild pink roses, you will have the perfect fragrance for our Queen.'

Pudding gazed sceptically at his friend. 'And where do I pluck this rare flower?'

'Why, in Ollie Ogre's garden,' declared Robin, in what he hoped was a nonchalant manner.

'In Ollie Ogre's garden?' repeated Pudding. 'You must be crazy. Everyone knows he has a squad of bluebottles defending his territory, and no-one has ever seen over the high walls into his garden!'

'Oh, I have, many times,' swaggered Robin. 'Ollie has the most marvellous selection of roses, but his pride and joy is the lilac rose. Its perfume is just out of this world! Come on, Pudding, we can walk up the hill, all in an afternoon.'

'You really think I can get some petals from the lilac rose?' queried the Pixie dazedly. 'Just a minute, where's my haversack, and, oh, I must take my tart with me.'

'Oh yes, don't forget your tart,' said his friend cheerily. 'We'll need *that*,' and he smiled a slow, mischievous smile.

The sun was hot and poor Pudding Pixie mopped his perspiring face with his cobweb hanky whilst clutching the tart firmly in his other hand. Up the hill they marched, quite a funny-looking couple – the little fat pixie and the trim little bird, hopping cheerily, at his side.

'Gosh, it's a long way to the top!' panted Pudding. 'What big stout walls Ollie has round his garden! However shall I get inside?'

'Just leave all that to me,' said his friend importantly. 'Just mind you don't drop the tart.'

Round the corner they trudged and there was a sweet little gatehouse manned by a couple of very officious hornets.

'Hi, where do you think you're going?' buzzed Holly Hornet.

'Oh, just taking a piece of tart to Ollie,' trilled Robin.

'My, that *does* look delicious,' hummed his friend Herbie Hornet.

'Break off a piece of tart,' ordered Robin. 'I'm sure these two guards could do with some sustenance!'

Reluctantly, Pudding broke off a generous piece. Whilst Holly and Herbie were ravenously devouring it the little bird was urging his friend down the path towards the rosebeds.

'What a gorgeous sight,' breathed Pudding. 'Oh, and look, there's that wonderful lilac rose!'

'Hurry,' implored Robin, 'before the bluebottles swoop down on us.'

But too late; an angry swarm of the big flies was already upon them.

'Quick, throw down the last piece of tart!'

The pixie didn't need telling twice. The amazed bluebottles stopped suddenly and dropped onto the luscious tart.

'Hurry, hurry,' tweeted Robin, 'help me pluck the

lilac petals.'

Pudding opened up his haversack and together they filled it with the fragrant petals.

'Come on, come on,' implored the little bird, 'we must get past the gatehouse before the guards have finished their tart.'

'My wonderful strawberry tart,' murmured the pixie.

'You can always make another one,' chided Robin.

'So I can,' mused Pudding. 'I think I'll make a cherry pie and we'll eat it together!'

'Come on, Pudding Pixie, let's run, or do you think your wings might carry you up and over these walls?'

'I'm sure I've lost lots of weight climbing up this awful hill,' declared Pudding. 'Let me fasten my haversack firmly in place. Now with a one, two and a three, away we go,' and, to his great surprise, he soared effortlessly over the garden wall!

Of course, he *had* noticed a few bluebottles coming in his direction!

Robin flew alongside, admiring. 'Just think, Pudding, if we climbed this hill once a week, we'd soon have you nice and slim!'

'No chance,' cried the pixie. 'I wouldn't need a nice big mushroom house if I was a skinny elf, and I want to have a bigger and better oven to bake delicious pies. I'd like to set up a bakery to sell goodies to all Fairyland. But, maybe, once a month we'll go on a hike together, Robin.'

'Don't forget to pick some wild roses,' reminded the little bird. 'Here's a lane full of bushes.' Gently they floated down and spent quite a time filling the haversack to bursting point.

All night long Pudding watched over his mixture of rose petals, and his own special magic liquid. At sunrise a lovely fragrance filled his little house. He hadn't any wonderful bottle to use but filled an old jam jar with the amber liquid.

The pixie didn't dare leave his precious scent till the day of the competition. Robin hopped by to tell him the latest news and to nibble luscious bits of fruit cake.

'Ollie Ogre's hopping mad about his lilac rose. I believe he won't give his hornets any holidays this year. Mind you, I've heard a whisper that they would like to put in an order for some of your jam tarts, Pudding!'

'Fancy that,' smirked the pixie. 'Perhaps I will toss them a piece of tart now and then when we hike up the hill.'

Saturday came and what excitement in Fairyland! Rows and rows of lovely bottles stood on a long table. Everyone laughed when they saw a common jam jar, but they didn't laugh when Queen Andrea proclaimed Pudding Pixie the winner! What a marvellous time Pudding and Robin had at the ball! Robin sat on the pixie's shoulder as he escorted the Queen and bowed low for the first dance.

And what about Sammy Sprite who was the cause of all this? He was found out, of course, and suitably punished. Guess who had to use up the Queen's horrid pond-water scent? And guess who smelled so awful no-one would go anywhere near him!

PUCK THE PAINTER

Puck, the pixie painter, whistled merrily. What a splendid day it was. A lovely blue sky and warm sunshine, but not too hot; just right for doing his yearly job of re-gilding the Fairy Queen's golden coach. With deft fingers he wielded his paintbrush this way and that, slowing down over the difficult part – the delightful edging of little stars.

'Hi there!' called Perry Pixie, 'how's the painting going? Don't forget the Fairy Queen is paying a visit to King Wizard, the day after tomorrow. Do you think the paint will be dry by then? You've left it a bit late, haven't you, this time?'

'Good gracious!' exclaimed Puck. 'I'd truly forgotten. I thought I'd have heaps of time to prepare the coach for our Queen's Jubilee celebrations next month! Oh, dearie me, I will have to hurry.'

He stopped his whistling and his face grew long with worry and concentration. Whatever had made him forget the state visit? The Queen had another coach, not so grand, but quite prettily decorated with lots of painted flowers, but she always liked to impress the King. There was quite a bit of rivalry between them both. They tried to outmatch one another with their magic and spells. Puck stuck out his chin determinedly. She *would* have her favourite coach if he had anything to do with it. He'd work the clock round he would! What a pity he didn't know the powerful magic spell which would finish his work for him! Still, that would be laziness. The Queen was very down on lazy pixies and fairies!

He sighed and rubbed his aching wrist. He would just finish this wheel, then pop along for a drink of nectar with his friends. He'd paint the other wheels afterwards. Ah, that was done nicely! He stepped back to amire his handiwork. How the paint shone and glittered in the sunshine!

Hurriedly he wiped his hands and flew off to find Perry and his other pixie chums. There they were, lying in the shade of a creamy mushroom.

'Come on Puck,' shouted Perry, 'we've saved a nice big cup of nectar for you. Sit yourself down and have a rest.'

'Oh, that's lovely,' sighed Puck. 'Painting does make you thirsty.'

'How come you forgot about the state visit?' asked Pinkie Pixie. 'Didn't the Queen send you a work notice?'

'Not this time,' said Puck earnestly, 'but I really should have put it in my diary myself. I'd better get back to work – I've still lots to do.'

Regretfully he rose from his mossy seat and flew back to the golden coach. My, how the gold did shine – even from a distance, everywhere seemed to dazzle – even the *ground* . . . ! It *was* the ground, covered in gold paint. Someone had spilled all his precious paint. He knew he had put the lid on before he left. It must have been deliberate. How could someone be so mean and spiteful?

What he didn't know was that a naughty goblin from King Wizardland had upset his paint. He was in fact tittering away in the treetops nearby. That very same naughty goblin had tweaked the work-note from the postman. The goblin was very fond of his master, King Wizard, and very jealous of Queen Sunshine. She wasn't going to turn up in the golden coach if he could help it. Wouldn't his master be pleased when he knew what he had done!

Puck covered his face with his hands and moaned softly. He knew there was no more paint in the storeroom. The elves needed a lot of time and a special ingredient to concoct the gold paint. He knew they had started on the task, but the paint wouldn't be ready for ages yet. What was he to do? He would never hold his head up again. Gloomily he sat down, not even bothering to try and clean up the glittering mess.

'Heigh ho!' trilled a little bird. 'What do I see, some lovely gold paint? I'll get a leaf-full and decorate my nest. Won't I be grand?'

'Just don't let it get on your feathers or you'll never fly again,' warned Puck.

Reggie Rabbit bounded by. 'Oh, I'm going to have a beautiful golden bobtail,' he said, and without more ado he swished his bob in the paint.

'You'll be an easy target for the hunters,' warned Puck.

'Oh, dear, I never thought of that,' worried Reggie.

Puck was desolate. No good at all would come of this. He'd better try and clean it all up. So with a sad heart he did his best with rags and then sprinkled moss over the whole thing.

Oswald Owl blinked down at Puck. 'What are you going to do now?'

The pixie looked surprised. 'What *can* I do?'

27

'Well, don't just sit there fuming,' hooted Oswald sternly. 'Go and find some more paint!'

'And just where would that be?' said Puck angrily.

'Why, out in the land of the humans, of course. They've got plenty. It's just knowing where to go.'

Puck brightened up. 'How do I get there, Oswald?'

'Oh, ask the South Wind to take you there tomorrow morning. Fly to the top of the highest tree and wait till the dawn breaks. Good luck!'

He flew away leaving Puck just a little lonely. He shook himself. The thing to do was to be practical. He cleaned up a large empty pot with a tight-fitting lid and put it, with a couple of rags and a wooden spoon, into his haversack. Then Puck added a handful of berries in a bag. Goodness knows how long he'd be away! Now for a good night's sleep. He wound up his dandelion clock and soon fell fast asleep on his thistledown bed.

It seemed no time at all before the little pixie was awakened from a deep sleep. He didn't feel much like eating, but decided it was a good idea. With a cup of camomile tea inside him, and some bread and honey, he felt better and was soon on his way.

No-one was about. How quiet everything was, but how beautiful too! He must do this again sometime. Puck flew higher and higher. Really he had never before flown so high! He was quite breathless when he landed at the peak of a poplar tree.

'Mind where you're going!' twittered a blackbird peevishly. 'Whatever are you doing – up so early *and* so high, too?'

'Off to get some paint!' exclaimed Puck, now quite excited and optimistic.

'All aboard for Humanland,' sighed the South Wind gustily. 'Just let me blow you along.'

Puck jumped into the stream of warm air and swam along effortlessly. It was rather nice, this. Just the first jump off the tree was a bit scary.

Faster and faster they went. Puck would have liked to look around him more, but all he could see were sunbeams and fluffy bits of cloud.

'Which part do you want?' sighed the Wind.

'Well – er – have you any ideas where gold paint is to be had?' asked the pixie.

'Gold paint?' echoed the South Wind. 'You'll need houses for that. The humans paint their houses all colours – red, pink, brown, green, yellow, blue and black – never gold. Still, I *have* seen gold paint on some doors. You'll just have to hunt around.'

With that he swooped lower and lower till Puck could see gigantic houses looming up. This really was frightening!

'When shall I see you again?' he asked the Wind. 'I do want to return to Fairyland as quickly as possible to finish painting the coach.'

'Catch my sister, the North Wind. She'll be returning at twelve o'clock. Fly to the top of the church steeple, over there.'

Puck looked up and down the street. No sign of any gold paint here. The houses were beautifully painted in red, or yellow or green. He flew up to one front door. Yes, here was a shiny gold knob. He examined it with a puzzled frown. How hard it was! What he needed was to see a human actually painting. That was it! Did they paint often? he wondered. The pixie wrinkled his nose and adjusted his special small feelers. Aha, he *could* smell paint! Off he flew. It came from a long, low building. He peeped in through a

30

window. Lots of girls and boys were putting all colours of paint on big white pieces of paper. They all had little pots in a box. Of course, to him, the pots were simply enormous!

One little girl looked up. 'Oh, look, Karen,' she said, 'what a lovely butterfly!'

Puck was indignant. Fancy likening him to a butterfly! A bit despondent, he flew on to a bush, and wrinkled his feelers. Just supposing there were lots of these long, low buildings; he'd never find any gold paint there. It seemed only to be on the front doors of houses.

A dragonfly came zooming up. 'Lost your way, Pixie? How come you're in Humanland?'

'Could you help me?' begged Puck. 'I desperately need some gold paint. Have you seen any, Desmond Dragonfly?'

'There's a man painting a house a mile away. Hop on my back, I'll take you there; I nearly got some paint stuck on my beautiful wings! I'll drop you off, but not too close!' He shuddered as he remembered his near disaster.

The little pixie was jubilant. Sure enough, a big human was painting a house a heavenly shade of blue! 'Wait, Desmond,' he shouted, 'it's only blue paint!' But Desmond was off, anxious to keep a special appointment of his own.

Puck stared dismally at the painter, who was putting the finishing touches to a little wicket gate. The man was muttering to himself. 'Now I wonder if I've time to do the front door before lunch!'

He disappeared into a shed and came out with a tin of paint and a smaller brush. The pixie nearly fainted with excitement. It *was* gold paint, it was *gold* paint! The man lifted up the lid and carefully painted the

31

number of the house. Then he painted round the edge of the door panels.

Puck carefully ladled some paint into his own pot and firmly fixed the lid. He hesitated. It seemed mean to take paint and not give anything for it, but the man had not even noticed the level of paint had dropped a little. What was that?

The man had put down his brush, and was taking a parcel from his coat. 'Cheese sandwiches again!' he muttered. 'How I wish I had a sirloin steak with all the trimmings *and* a nice, cold glass of lager!'

Puck danced with joy. He could always do lovely spells for other people, never for himself. He concentrated and, in no time at all, there was a large steak with chips, peas and mushrooms *and* a lovely cold drink, sitting on the doorstep!

'My, oh my, what's this?' chortled the man, but wasted no time in setting to and enjoying his amazing luck.

Puck flew off and was just in time to catch the North Wind back to Fairyland. Soon he was at work on the fairy coach, and by nightfall he had done the job thoroughly. He wasn't going to leave his paint-pot again. Oh, dear me, *no*! Let his hand ache and ache, he'd paint till the job was done. The pixie carefully locked the door of the shed where he had wheeled the coach the previous day and flew off home for a well-earned rest.

Wasn't the goblin surprised when Queen Sunshine turned up in her glittering coach the day after! He just couldn't understand it at all, at all.

MR SNOWMAN'S PARTY

David was excited. When he awoke the world was carpeted with a thick layer of lovely clean snow, just the right sort for making a wonderful snowman. He could hardly wait to eat his breakfast before donning his cheery red anorak and his black shiny wellingtons.

Out he clumped into the back garden, noting with relish the footprints in the virgin snow. Wistful little birds marked his progress and wondered if he would remember them, but they need not have worried, David was a kind little boy and he had his pockets full of delectable, soft crumbs. With a blue, wooden spade he cleared the bird table of its four-inch covering of snow, and carefully sprinkled the crumbs all around. As the birds flocked to eat their breakfast he shouted, 'I'm going to build a snowman. So stay and watch!'

'We will, we will,' they chorused in grateful chirps.

David worked very hard packing the snow together to form a solid body for Mr Snowman. He was glad Mummy had made him wear rubber gloves over his woollen ones. His hands were so cold, and his face was rosy from the keen air. At last the body was big enough and Robin plodded back to the kitchen for a
David

33

mug of hot chocolate to revive him.

'Have you four very large buttons for my snowman's front, Mummy?'

His mother went off to search through her button box and, sure enough, returned with four large shiny green buttons. These he pressed carefully into the chest of Mr Snowman. Now he must make a head and he rolled the snow round and round. Oh, it was hard work! Would it ever be big enough? Maybe he had been too ambitious and made the body too large.

Eventually, the ball of snow was just the right size and, with a sigh of satisfaction, he moulded it on top of the body. At last he had come to the really interesting part! Off he clumped to the kitchen door, feeling sorry to have to take off his wellingtons. It took simply ages to shake all the snow onto the mat.

'Have we an old scarf and a hat – oh, and a pipe, Mummy?'

'You'd better have a look in the old chest in the spare room,' she said, 'I'm busy baking.'

It was so interesting looking through the odd assortment of things that he took simply ages before he found an old bubble pipe, a bright pink scarf and a yellow and purple woolly cap. Goodness, what a lot of colours! Ah well, he couldn't wait any longer to dress up Mr Snowman. Out he rushed with his trophies.

'My goodness,' trilled one little sparrow. 'Do you see what I see, Jenny Wren? Whatever will Mr Snowman say tonight?' They giggled away and nearly fell off the fence!

David had brought two blue buttons for eyes, and he firmly rolled the snow and made quite a presentable nose. He made the mouth with a piece of twig and stuck in the blue bubble pipe. The green and purple cap and the shocking-pink scarf completed the picture. Really it was no wonder they had ended up in the chest. What colours! Mother came out to admire the wonderful, if clownish, snowman. David was delighted and, after a pat here and there, retired indoors, exhausted. 'I do hope it does not snow too much tonight,' he worried.

'It would take an awful lot of snow to cover your snowman,' laughed Mother. 'Now come and have some tea. Your father will be here soon, and think how surprised he'll be to see you've made a snowman all by yourself.'

That night the moon was full, and shed her lovely light over the snowclad land. Mr Snowman was a solitary and silent figure, but then a whisper came from the eaves of David's home. A tiny sparrow flew down on to the snowman's cap.

'Won't be long now,' he chirruped. 'Six of you fellows are coming over at midnight, and you can all have a grand party.'

'Oh, goody,' yawned Mr Snowman, and then remembering, 'my goodness what *will* they think of my cap and scarf?'

'Not to worry,' cheeped Mr Sparrow. 'My guess is that they too will be a funny sight!'

Out popped Jenny Wren, Bobby Blackbird and Speckie Thrush. Jenny Wren hopped onto the pipe and peered into its bowl as if in search of something tasty. The others admired the green buttons, then perched on the cap, waiting patiently.

Shuffle, shuffle, down the side of the house, majestically shifting from side to side, came the first guest, Bowler Snowman. Really, he did look well in his black bowler hat and with a black pipe. What

spoiled the effect was a rainbow-coloured shawl over his shoulders. Following close behind was Tiny Snowman – only half his size, but he looked cute dressed in a baby's old bonnet and shawl. Four more snowmen slid around the corner, and they did look a sight. One had on a man's Panama hat; another a lady's straw hat all trimmed with plastic red cherries; another had a furry hood with pom-poms, and the very last snowman sported a bright red and white school cap! David's snowman tried hard not to laugh – to think he had worried so about his own appearance! 'Hi, folks,' he shouted merrily, 'happy to see you. Let's have a lovely sliding party!'

Lots of birds chirped happily from the headgears of the snowmen. They dearly loved to slide, and, after all, however could a party have been organised without their help? Round and round the lawn shuffled the snowmen, till the snow lay hard and smooth and, with a joyous cry of 'We're off!' they slid around the bird table. Their feathered passengers squeaked with delight hanging on precariously. Lady Moon looked down and smiled on the happy scene. What *would* David have said about it all?

Breathlessly the snowmen stopped their antics and decided it was time to go their separate ways. They thanked Mr Snowman and shuffled off with their passengers. But Mr Snowman was worried – his cap had stuck on a branch. Perhaps there was something to be said for his woolly cap. Yes, decidedly his head was too cold! The little sparrow tried in vain to unhook it from the tree but, no use, so off he flew to join the others under the eaves.

David awoke early, and dashed to the window to see if his snowman was still there. Yes, of course he was, and the snow too, but what was that hanging on the branch? Fancy that – Mr Snowman's woolly cap! However did that get there? he pondered. Really the wind must have been quite strong during the night! Happily he hurried downstairs. Another lovely day to spend in the snow, but first he must retrieve the woolly cap. Mr Snowman didn't look quite right without it. Most definitely it suited him!

SUNNY SQUIRREL'S
AMAZING ADVENTURE

In the heart of a deep forest lived Sunny Squirrel. All tucked up in a cosy nest he dozed on and off all day through the snowy winter days. On this particular day he awoke feeling quite hungry.

'Oh, dear! Now where did I put those special walnuts? I quite fancy some. Let's see, last time I ate up my hazelnuts. That must have been a month ago. Good gracious! I do believe it's nearly Christmas.'

He popped his head outside and surveyed the scene. Snow plopped softly on his red-gold fur.

'Tee-hee,' chuckled Robin Redbreast, swinging to and fro, 'who's a dozy squirrel? It's Christmas Day tomorrow. Come on, let's have fun!'

Sunny yawned sleepily. 'Righto Robin, but first I must find my breakfast nuts.'

'Don't tell me you've forgotten where they are again,' laughed he. 'You really do need a diary. Why don't you ask Father Christmas for one?'

'That's an idea,' said Sunny, seriously. 'Do you think we'll ever see him, Robin?'

'Oh, I caught a glimpse of him one Christmas,' boasted he, airily. 'It was when I was on a visit to my cousin Rennie. Quite a splendid man, all dressed in red and white. Red is *so* right, don't you think?'

Here he looked down proudly at his own redbreast. Then he added, kindly, 'You look rather a nice colour too, Sunny. Your fur glows redly in the sun.'

'Now let's think, Sunny, have you dug up those nuts by the tall fir trees?'

'Oh, yes, I had those a few weeks ago.'

'What about the hole in the big oak tree?'

'No, those are hazelnuts. I rather fancied walnuts. I put them in a very safe place.'

'Too safe!' laughed Robin.

Sunny Squirrel groomed his beautiful bushy tail which he had used as a blanket to keep him warm. His tail was very useful. If he slipped on the icy branches it would unfurl like a parachute. 'Come with me, won't you, Robin. I've suddenly had a thought. I'm sure they're hidden near Big Rock.'

'Righto,' chirped his friend, 'let's be on our way.'

He spread his wings and the snow fell in a cloud onto Rollie Rabbit just passing beneath.

'What's the rush?' he grumbled. 'Just mind what you're doing!'

'Sunny Squirrel can't remember where his walnuts are,' twittered Robin.

'Just like him,' said Rollie. 'He spends months going to and fro with that little pouch of his, then he forgets where he's put his nuts. You want to ask Father Christmas for a new memory box. Ha, ha!' and off he bounced.

It was a lovely morning. The sky was blue and the sun sparkled on the freshly-fallen snow. Sunny swung among the branches, only coming to the ground when the trees were too far apart. Robin flitted to and fro, exchanging merry greetings with all his friends. 'There's a special treat on the bird table at

Rose Cottage,' chirped Gerald Greenfinch.

'Oh, goody! I could do with something,' said Robin. 'Come on, Sunny, perhaps there'll be something for you too.'

Sunny kept out of sight while Robin joined the other birds, and tucked into bacon rinds. Tits swung busily on nets full of nuts. Robin shouted, 'Tommy Tit, can you get me some peanuts? Our friend, Sunny Squirrel is famished!'

'Sure, sure,' sang Tommy, and he quickly darted back and forth till he had a little pile of them. Sunny was very grateful for the snack.

Soon they were on their way to Big Rock. 'Ah, yes, there's the special pine tree. I buried my walnuts there.'

With gusto, Sunny scrabbled in the ground while Robin watched with bright and beady eyes. Sure enough, the nuts were there. He put them in his little pouch and sat back exhausted. 'Like one, Robin?' he asked.

'Well, just a tiny piece,' said his friend.

Sunny munched happily till he was really full. 'There are still some left. I think I'll re-bury them, but not exactly in the same place. Someone may have been watching. Now let me see.' He scampered up and down the Big Rock. 'Ah, here is the very place! A deep crevice!'

Robin hopped along, determined to note the hiding place.

As Sunny pressed the nuts in a sudden and terrific thing happened. With a groaning and a creaking, a huge piece of rock slid back. Snow scattered all over poor Sunny, and Robin was nearly buried in it.

'I say, I say,' he croaked, 'whatever next!'

Sunny was horrified; he saw all his walnuts

disappearing down the hole. He peered in, then stepped inside. 'Come on, come on,' he said, shakily, 'don't desert me, Robin!'

Robin shook his feathers and tiptoed in. Down a passage they went, then round a corner and, whatever do you think they saw? You'll never guess! Why, lots and lots of toys of all kinds. In the roof of the cave were lots of little stars lighting up the scene. Lovely little dolls, brightly-coloured boxes, train sets, coloured crayons and piles of tinsel-covered packages.

'Ooh, how marvellous,' they both cried. 'Why it must be Father Christmas's store! I wonder why he's not here sorting it all out,' pondered Sunny. 'Perhaps,' he said shyly, 'he's forgotten where he put the presents!'

'Could be,' giggled Robin. 'I daresay he has lots of stores. I know he needs scores of helpers on Christmas Eve. All the wood fairies help him, you know.'

Sunny Squirrel looked worried. 'Just think of all those little boys and girls who will be disappointed on Christmas morning if they don't receive these lovely gifts. What shall we do about it, Robin?'

'Well,' said his friend, slowly, 'we could go and find Father Christmas, my cousin Rennie will help. He lives quite a long way from here. Do you think you feel up to it, Sunny?'

'Of course, I've filled my pouch with delicious fat walnuts to eat on the way and, guess what, Robin, I picked up some lovely cake-crumbs for you. A small Christmas gift, you know!'

'Let's be on our way then,' cried Robin.

They carefully found their way to the opening and, after a bit of puffing and blowing, Sunny managed to shut the rock door.

Off they sped through the forest, the little bird flying ahead and carolling directions to his friend. Deep in the forest they journeyed. Robin suddenly chirped, 'Hi, Rennie, how are you?'

'My, my, fancy seeing *you*,' whistled Rennie. 'I thought I wouldn't be seeing you till the spring! Why, if it isn't Sunny Squirrel too! I thought you'd be fast asleep!'

'We've made an exciting discovery, Rennie. We've found some of Santa's toys. Could you direct us to his home?'

'Sure, I'll take you there myself, but first why don't we have lunch? You'll feel so refreshed with the break.'

So they all sat back on a bank of green velvet moss and finished their meal with a long drink from a clear spring.

'This way,' carolled Rennie. On and on they sped through the snow-laden pines. Snow flurries marked their progress. 'Not long now, I hope,' panted Sunny.

'Just around the corner,' shouted Rennie.

Sure enough, they came upon a lovely white cottage nearly hidden by the snow. It nestled beneath a huge rock.

'There are caves in there,' whispered Rennie, 'where Father Christmas makes his toys.'

Sunny Squirrel knocked on the little red door. 'Is Father Christmas at home?' he enquired of a tiny elf.

'He's busy in the loading cave,' came the reply.

'We've got some important news for him,' chirped Robin. 'Do you think we could disturb him? We know he's very busy.'

44

The little elf took a big, black key from his apron pocket, and off they all trooped. The cave doors were numbered 1, 2, 3, 4 and 5. Two were storerooms, two workshops and number 5 was the loading cave. Our friends shivered with excitement. Fancy, they were actually going to talk with Father Christmas!

Inside number 5 was a wonderful sight! Fairies dressed in red and white fur caps and boots, stacked the sledges high with toys and parcels. Father Christmas himself was a magnificent figure in red velvet with lots of white fur and shiny black boots. He immediately caught sight of our trio. 'Ho, ho who have we here? What brings you out so far, Sunny Squirrel?'

Shyly, Sunny told his story.

'Good gracious! What a good thing you found those toys. Someone broke into my storeroom not long ago and stole them. I knew I couldn't give everybody all they asked for this Christmas. I've been so worried, I don't like disappointing children. Where did you say you found the toys? A cave in Big Rock? Aha – I know who stole them – the five green goblins! I saw them skulking round my caves.'

Father Christmas stroked his beard reflectively. 'I'll be able to give you a sleigh ride back home if you wait till darkness falls. You can help me load the stolen toys and I'll drop you off wherever you fancy.'

'Oh, yes,' chorused the three friends. 'How marvellous to be with Santa on Christmas Eve!'

'Now go and have a rest and my elf will give you tea to refresh you.'

So the trio sat in Santa's cottage, admiring his carved wooden furniture and his furry rugs and cushions.

The time passed quickly and soon a knock came

on the door and it was time to go. What a glorious sight met their eyes! Sleighs full of wonderful toys and parcels, tinsel-wrapped. Reindeer pawing the ground, anxious to be off, and lots of elves dressed like Santa, holding the reins. Sunny, Robin and Rennie felt very proud as they were escorted to Father Christmas's sledge. There they settled comfortably for the ride. Swiftly they skimmed the snow, the sleigh bells sweetly ringing.

'This way, Father Christmas!' directed Robin, and soon they were outside Big Rock. Sunny opened the door, and was nearly knocked over by a green goblin. He turned round and dived back into the cave. Father Christmas and our friends dashed inside and saw the goblins trying to hide behind stacks of toys. In the twinkling of an eye Santa reached out and popped the five into his big sack and tied it up!

'You naughty little boys! I'll make sure you don't trouble us in Oak Woods any more. Come on, Sunny, help me move all this out onto the sledge.'

Robin and Rennie helped by carrying the feather-light baubles for Christmas trees and tiny packets of sweets and miniature dollies. Eventually the cave was empty and Santa strode to the door and dumped the sack behind him on the sledge.

'Ooh, do let us out, Santa. We'll never do it again. We'll be good!'

But Santa took no notice – he was going to drop the sack when he was far, far away. In fact, he dropped the goblins in the garden of Witch Wicky. What a Christmas present for her! She might very well turn them into frogs!

As for our friends, they never stopped telling everyone about their wonderful ride. Rennie spent Christmas Day with Robin and they were forever admiring themselves in the budgie mirrors Santa had given them. Sunny was so tired he slept right through till spring, all cuddled up in a scarlet cape and hat, and clutching a little green diary in his paws!

HOW THE WIZARD LOST HIS MAGIC

What excitement and merriment there was in Joyland! Princess Angeline was soon to be married to young and handsome Prince David of Sunland. There was to be an impressive ceremony in the Cathedral and a sumptuous feast and ball afterwards. Everyone was happy and busy, for now there were only six days left before the day itself. People scurried around cleaning, polishing and decorating everything in sight. Up at the Palace, the Princess flitted to and fro, discussing arrangements with her many bridesmaids, and the King and Queen were in a whirl as they attended to a thousand and one details.

Yet there was one sour person in Joyland – Wizard Weevil. Although he was usually quite a reasonable man, now he was simply furious that his son, Rupert, was not to marry the Princess. Rupert did not mind too much, but he had decided to go away on a long holiday till the wedding was over. Wizard Weevil stomped up and down in his castle.

Suddenly a roguish smile crept across his face. 'That's what I'll do!' he exclaimed triumphantly. He rang for his manservant. 'Bring Goblin Glee immediately, I have some important work for him to do.'

In no time at all Goblin Glee was before him,

listening to his master's instructions. 'Here's a bag.' He produced a tiny drawstring pouch. 'I wish you to drop its contents into the well which supplies the city. Every day, till the day of the wedding is passed, I shall require you to do this. You will find the bags in the tower storeroom, and each will have this word on the label: FORGETFUL. Be sure to drop the powder in before the people come to draw water for the day.'

'That shall be done, my Wizard.' Glee bowed and hastened on his way.

'Tee-hee,' laughed Weevil, 'that should spoil the wedding. They'll all be so forgetful and lazy, I'm going to enjoy myself watching the confusion!' He himself had his own special well in the castle grounds. Wasn't he glad he had!

Next morning, bright and early, Bobby Blackbird was amazed to see Goblin Glee tiptoeing to the edge of the well. 'Good gracious, what's he doing here? I thought Wizard Weevil had a well of his own; he says the water is much superior to this. Now what is Glee doing? Why, he's tipping a bag of powder down the well! Really, I bet he's up to some mischief. Now he's running away. I wonder what was in that bag. How I wish I could tell the people not to drink from the well today. Oh, dear! I must tell someone. I'll gather all my friends.'

Soon his melodious song had brought dozens of birds to his tree. 'Don't drink any water that has been taken from the well. Fly to the Blue Lake instead.'

The birds twittered away, discussing the antics of Goblin Glee. Then off they went to perch on windowsills and peep through windows to see what exactly would happen when the people had drunk their first cup of tea. Bobby Blackbird flapped

50

frantically against the glass as a dear, little friend of his, Pamela, picked up a glass of water, but all she said was, 'Oh, dear, poor blackie-bird, he wants some water!' And off she hurried to fill the birds' drinking pot.

Up and down the city the birds perched at vantage points to watch and wait. 'The shops are late opening today,' murmured Willie Wagtail.

'Look, Mistress Mary hasn't even washed up yet,' chirped Jenny Wren, 'and she's forgotten to put out some crumbs for me!'

Sammy Starling said shrilly, 'Look how slowly they're walking in the streets, and every few minutes they sit down!'

'That must be it,' twittered Bobby Blackbird, 'the powder upsets everyone, it makes them lazy and forgetful. Nothing will be ready on the wedding day. In fact, there may never be a wedding day, everyone will have forgotten all about it.'

'Not Prince David,' cheeped Jenny Wren, wisely, 'but won't he be disappointed when he finds nothing is ready?'

'We *must* do something, but what?' chirped Bobby. 'I know, let's all go and find Oswald Owl, he'll tell us what to do.'

Off they flew and found Oswald looking as if he too had taken forgetful-water, but, of course, he was much too wise for that. He had been up all night and knew precisely what was going on, everywhere.

'I thought I would have to round you all up,' he whooed sleepily. 'What a to-do, but easily remedied.'

'How, Ossie?' enquired Bobby anxiously.

'Simple, isn't it?' whooed the owl. 'You must get the other bags of forgetful powder and drop them in the

Wizard's well.'

'How simply fantastic,' twittered all the birds. 'Weevil and Glee will forget all about their plan. Ha, ha, ha!'

'On your way, my friends,' whooed Ossie. 'Your human friends will soon recover, provided no more powder is dropped in their well water.'

The birds gathered in the woods around the castle and planned their campaign. 'Ossie says the bags are kept in the tower room. There's a nice little window someone can squeeze through, but it must be done well before dawn,' said Bobbie, solemnly.

'I'm sure I can be lots of help. I'm so small,' twittered Jenny Wren.

'But do you think you can carry a bag?' asked Tommy Thrush.

'Well, perhaps if you would help me, dear Gracie Goldcrest?'

'Of course,' came the soft answer. So the birds paired off, little ones promising to carry the bags from the tower room to the window, and the big birds preparing to catch them and take them to the Wizard's well.

None of the birds slept much that night. They were anxious not to oversleep, although Oswald Owl had promised to give a long 'Too-whit, too-whoo' when it was time to be off. Lots of beady eyes peeped from trees and bushes. Then there was a rustle and a subdued flapping. All the creatures of the woods and fields were absolutely amazed to see a flock of birds, all kinds and sizes, sweep upwards towards the Wizard's castle.

'My, oh, my!' squeaked Sticky Stoat. 'That I should live to see such a sight! Am I dreaming or did I eat too much supper?'

Once they had reached the trees near the Round Tower, the birds waited and scanned their surroundings. No-one seemed to be about; no-one had noticed their arrival. Now came the tricky part. First to go was Jenny Wren and her partner, Grace Goldcrest. With ease they slipped through the open window and tweeted softly at the display of bottles and bags. Now they must be sure to get the right ones. Ah, the Wizard was very methodical; all were arranged in alphabetical order. Jenny and Grace shuddered over one bottle marked POISON, and then giggled over one marked LOVE. Ah, here were the bags they wanted – about ten bags in all. Jenny flew to the window. 'Coo-ee, be ready to catch them.'

Tommy and Tessie Thrush rushed to be first. Then came Bobby and Bessie Blackbird, followed by Sammy and Sandie Starling. Between them Jenny and Gracie carried the bag and, with a great heave, managed to push it over the sill to the waiting birds. They flew to the trees where Wendy and Willie Wagtail, Susie and Stevie Sparrow and Rosie and Robin Redbreast were waiting to fly the remaining distance to Wizard Weevil's well.

'Might as well take all the bags,' tweeted Jenny, 'then no more damage can be done.'

The whole operation was done methodically and quickly. Bernie Bullfinch and Tiny Tit and his family kept a look-out, darting round the castle to see if anyone stirred. Jenny and Gracie were very tired, but so thrilled they were the only ones who could have made the venture a success. Wizard Weevil only kept one window slightly open. He didn't want his precious potions stolen!

At the wellside the birds were busy removing the

drawstrings from the bags. Then with a 'one-two-three, away we go,' they tipped the 'lazy and forgetful' powder into the water. How tired they all were after the ten bags had been emptied!

'Let's rest awhile,' chirped Jenny.

'No, we must be on our way. Time enough for rest back home. We don't want the Wizard to suspect anything. He and Goblin Glee simply must drink this water,' cautioned Bobby Blackbird.

Just then a dark shape loomed up. 'Why if it isn't Rollie Rook!'

'Thought I'd give Jenny and Gracie a lift. Knew they'd be tired.'

'Oh, thank you, Rollie. How simply splendid! We thought you were away for the night.'

'Just got back and heard the news,' croaked Rollie.

Oswald Owl had promised to keep a watch on the well, early morning. Would people be even too tired to come for water? No, they were late but seemed more perky today. The effects of the drug were wearing off. The exhausted birds had a well-earned rest, but came to relieve Ollie at noon. No Goblin Glee turned up. Perhaps the Wizard was making more powder? Well, they had better send someone to find out.

Bobbie Blackbird circled the castle. All was still. He peeped in the windows. Everyone was fast asleep! The remains of breakfast were on the long dining table. In the kitchen were two buckets of water. One was nearly empty. 'Oh, goody-goody – our plan has succeeded!'

He hastened to tell his friends and they all sang and sang with happiness. Next day, the people were quite energetic. 'We really must get on with our preparations for the wedding. I wonder what happened on

Tuesday?' said the King and Queen. 'Can't seem to think what we did.'

'I guess it's all the excitement,' smiled the Princess. 'I can't remember either!'

Bobby Blackbird flew up to the castle once more. This time the servants were awake, but it was obvious they were feeling lazy. Wizard Weevil and Goblin Glee were just the same and, because they had drunk so deeply of the forgetful water, the Wizard couldn't even remember how to make any more powder and Goblin Glee couldn't be bothered to make mischief any more!

PUSSY AND THE MAGIC STONE

What a to-do there was in Happiland! Queen Esmeralda had lost the wishing stone from her jewelled crown! How would she manage without it? How to conduct the affairs of her realm? What a lot of hard work she would need to do instead! Among other things, she particularly wanted to wish for splendid weather for her daughter's wedding. Everyone in Happiland enjoyed the best of housing and delicious food, but they were just a bit lazy. If anything disastrous happened they had only to ask Queen Esmeralda and she would put everything all right again. However, if too many wishes were made in a short period of time the beautiful red stone would fade to a dull pink. Then the Queen had to wait till the gorgeous red glow returned. So, you see, everyone had to exert themselves from time to time, which was a good thing; they didn't become too lazy!

Queen Esmeralda felt guilty. She had been so tired, after dancing all night at her daughter's engagement ball, that she had just flopped into bed without removing her crown. In the morning she took it off to comb her hair and, horror of horrors, the red gem had gone!

'Calm yourself, Esmeralda,' she spoke to herself sharply. 'The magic stone will be in the bedclothes or on the floor.'

Speedily she removed the satin sheets and peeped under the bed. There was no sign of the wishing stone. 'Ah, I know, it will have fallen into the pillow case,' and she eagerly felt inside. The stone was not there either!

Esmeralda's godmother had bequeathed the gem, with its special powers, to her, and had told the Queen never to disclose to anyone what magic it possessed. Oh, supposing someone had found her stone and happened to wish whilst holding it. What a thought! She would never recover the gem. All the same, she had to declare it was lost, or no-one would look for it!

Herbie, her lovely black and white pussy, rubbed round Esmeralda's legs as if to say, 'Never mind my Queen.'

'Oh, Pussy,' she wailed, 'I *am* in a state!'

Herbie mewed and purred softly as she stroked his velvety fur.

A knock came on the bedroom door, and in stepped a lady-in-waiting with the Queen's breakfast tray. She gasped as she noted the disorder of the room with sheets and pillow-cases strewn around. 'Your Majesty, whatever . . . ?'

'Oh, Mariana, I have lost one of the jewels in my crown! The red stone!'

'Never mind,' soothed Mariana, 'we can soon put that right. I'll inform the Court jewellers straight away!'

'If it were so simple,' thought the Queen. 'All the same, Mariana, I would like a proclamation to go out. Everyone in the land must search for it. I will give . . .' Here she hesitated; she mustn't offer too great a reward, or someone would become suspicious. 'I will reward the finder with one of my special gold coins.'

'As you wish,' said her lady-in-waiting. 'I will inform the Town Crier immediately.'

As soon as the door closed, Queen Esmeralda darted to and fro in a desperate attempt to locate the magic stone. Footsteps sounded outside her door and she quickly jumped into bed and made a start on her breakfast.

Mariana entered and brought Pussy's special tray with his fish and milk. 'It's a lovely day, ma'am. Now eat up your breakfast, and don't go worrying about that red stone. You will soon have another to replace it.'

'Yes, of course, Mariana,' said Esmeralda faintly.

Herbie looked up from his breakfast; he knew his mistress was upset. The next few days found everyone in Happiland scurrying around seeking the red stone. The Palace ballroom was searched from floor to ceiling, but to no avail.

Queen Esmeralda was busy. She couldn't rely on her precious stone to shorten her duties and remove problems. Still, she was quite satisfied with the way she overcame them all, and reflected that maybe she *had* become a little lazy. All the same, she hoped she wouldn't be so busy for too long – she wasn't as young as she used to be!

Herbie was puzzled. He had quite an entertaining existence with the family of mice who lived under the floorboards in the Queen's bedroom. Really he was too well fed to be much of a nuisance to them, but he loved to chase them around. Where had they been recently? Pussy put his left eye to a hole in the skirting board, and peered down.

'Good gracious!' Could he believe what he saw?

Miniature wine bottles lay on their side, obviously empty, and there were whole cheeses too. Two or three mice were teetering around and quite a lot were slumped together in a corner. They were *drunk*! How on earth could they have obtained all those luxuries? No wonder they hadn't been upstairs for biscuits – they were too well fed! Queen Esmeralda always had a nice supply of chocolate wholemeal biscuits in her bedside cabinet. She loved to nibble them in bed!

Ah, what was that, gleaming in the far corner? Could it be . . . ? Indeed, yes, it *was* the magic stone. Somehow, someone had found out about its magic properties! No doubt the gem was loose in the crown and it had rolled off the bed and right into the hole.

Herbie's chief adversary, Marmaduke Mouse, approached. He was not so silly as the rest. He wasn't drunk, and he had soon noticed the yellow eye gleaming and blocking the entrance.

'Hello Herbie,' he squeaked, 'don't you come and upset our lovely party. It will go on for ever and ever! Your mistress has lost her precious stone has she? She'll never get it back, you know. Oh, dear me *no*; it's far too useful. What marvellous luck it rolled into our mousehole! Mind you, we had to work hard to move it right in!'

Pussy grimaced. 'Wait till I get hold of you.'

'Oh, no,' squeaked Marmaduke. 'I'm going to get rid of you right now,' and stepping daintily on to the red stone he cried, 'move Pussie Herbie miles away into the Enchanted Forest!'

No sooner said than done. Herbie was alarmed to find himself looking up at tall fir trees.

'Help!' squealed a rabbit. 'Where did that pussy come from?' Herbie looked around. Nothing but trees and bluebells for miles and miles! Still, they were ever so pretty. Might as well have a little snooze before it was time to explore. All this magic was *so* tiring for a fellow!

Karen was picking bluebells and, so busy was she that, at first, she didn't notice Herbie. When she did she let out a cry of delight. 'What a lovely pussy!' Perhaps he would come home for a saucerful of milk.

Herbie stretched luxuriously. Now, what was on his mind? Ah, the red stone. But who was this, stroking him so gently? What a delightful little girl!

'Hello,' he miaowed, and stepped daintily after her as she skipped down the woodland path.

'We live in a sweet, little whitewashed cottage. Look, you can see the smoke coming from the chimney over there at the top of the fir trees. Blackie will be so pleased to see you; she's my pussy and she's very old.'

Herbie was a bit apprehensive. Supposing the old tabby didn't care for him? Still, he was getting hungry, he might as well go along with things.

Through a little white gate, up a red path bordered with pretty flowers, they went.

'I'm home, Mummy,' shouted Karen, 'and I've got a big surprise!'

Mother came running to the door. 'Why, whoever is this? Where have you come from my little friend?'

Herbie miaowed, but of course she couldn't understand him. All the same, he could understand *her* language. He often wondered why humans and animals couldn't converse. Surely life would be the sweeter if only they could? Ah, who was this, sauntering up behind? Of course, Blackie!'

'Miaow-miaow, I know *you*. You are the Queen's

cat, I saw you in town once. Whatever are you doing *here*?'

'I'll tell you later,' mewed Herbie. 'It's quite a long story.'

'Well, come on in,' smiled Karen's mother. 'Karen, get some milk for your new friend.'

Herbie gave his full attention to the lovely creamy milk and, having washed a few drops from his whiskers, he settled down comfortably on a rag mat in front of the fire. Karen's mother bent to stroke him and found the disc that hung round his neck.

'Why, Karen, we have a very important visitor here! Guess who he is – he's the Queen's very own pussy cat.'

'Herbie!' The little girl clapped her hands with joy. 'Oh, Blackie, isn't it an honour to have him here!'

Blackie mewed politely and said, 'We'll have a nice long chat tonight when everyone is in bed.'

'Don't you go out courting?' demanded Herbie.

'What, at my age? There aren't any cats round about here. The nearest cottage is ten miles away.'

'Ten miles,' echoed Herbie. 'What a dull life you must lead.'

'Oh, it's been pleasant enough,' miaowed Blackie, 'lots of rabbits to chase, you know!'

Karen's mother was considering how she should take Herbie back to the Queen. 'It must be 20 miles,' she mused. 'We'll have to take the cart and have Nobbie draw it. I'll give him some lovely new carrots, so he'll be full of zip!'

Soon everyone was in bed. Karen's father was away for the night. He had travelled to the nearby village where he hoped to sell the carved wooden toys he had made. He had taken their rather smart carriage with Floss, the pony, to draw it.

The two cats curled cosily together in a blanket-lined basket. 'Now tell me all about everything,' demanded Blackie eagerly.

Herbie lost no time in telling of his adventure. 'Isn't it maddening! I know where my mistress's magic stone is, but I don't know how to tell her! I've tried sitting by the hole, and all she says is, 'That's right, Pussy, keep those mice away!' Once she even bent down and had a look, but the mice had moved the stone further away, and anyway, she hasn't *my* superior eyesight!' Here he fluffed himself importantly.

Blackie was silent for a long time. 'Can I trust you, Herbie?'

'Of course,' mewed her friend. 'Well, will you promise me one request if I show you how to talk with your mistress?' Herbie interrupted with an incredulous miaow. 'You must be magic yourself, Blackie, if you can manage *that*!'

'A little,' simpered his friend. 'Once upon a time I belonged to a wizard; I picked up a thing or two!'

Herbie was impressed.

'Tonight,' she mewed, I will go out into the woods and bring a special herb. If you drink its juice with your milk, for one whole day you will be able to converse with human beings, but you mustn't talk till you see Queen Esmeralda.'

'Incredible,' purred Herbie. 'What do I do for you?'

'You must promise faithfully to bring a kitten for Karen. I am too old to have kittens, and she will be so upset when I die. I would like one of your kittens, Herbie.'

Herbie purred. 'Yes, yes, my dear friend Tabby Topaz has four delightful kittens, They will be old enough to leave their mother in about two or three weeks' time. They are the very image of me!'

'That's all right then,' sighed Blackie. 'Now for my excursion into the woods.'

'I'll come too,' offered Herbie.

'Sorry, my friend, I promised the wizard not to disclose where this special bush grows.'

Herbie contented himself with gazing into the embers of the wood fire. It didn't seem long before Blackie was back with a sprig of green leaves which she soaked in Herbie's milk. 'There, drink it up.'

'Tasteless,' thought he, 'and the leaves look just the same as any ordinary leaves.'

He lapped it all up, then settled himself for a long, cosy sleep.

They were awakened by a clatter of pots from the kitchen and soon a delicious smell of bacon pervaded the cottage. Karen came downstairs looking pretty in a rose-sprigged dress. 'Good morning, Pussies, would you like some fish for breakfast?' Off she went to the larder.

Herbie suddenly had a thought. 'Blackie,' he miaowed, 'how do I give the kitten to Karen?'

'Yes, I have thought about that,' replied his friend. 'In a few weeks' time the fair is coming to town. Karen's father will be selling his toys there and Karen and her mother will be coming too to enjoy the festivities. They pass over a little humpbacked bridge just outside town. Be waiting there at lunch time. My guess is they will have a picnic by the stream there.'

'Good,' exclaimed Herbie, 'I will be there in good time with the kitten.'

After breakfast Karen's mother harnessed Nobbie to the cart. Karen picked up Herbie. 'Say goodbye to Blackie.'

Herbie was sad that his friend could not accompany them. 'I can't stand the jolting over the stones these days,' Blackie said regretfully. 'Take care, my friend, so happy to have met you.'

Off they went, having first placed a note to Karen's daddy on the kitchen table and, also put a good supply of juicy carrots in the cart. Herbie was quiet; he didn't dare utter a miaow to the humans in case words came from his mouth. He did hope the herb had worked its magic; soon enough he would know!

On the way they had a lovely picnic in the wayside woods and Nobbie was glad of a rest. Early in the afternoon they came in sight of the palace turrets rising above the town. 'Won't Queen Esmeralda be surprised to see us!' chuckled Karen excitedly.

The sentry at the lodge-gates was amazed to see Herbie sitting in the cart. He waved them through the gates and soon the little donkey-cart and its occupants were at the very door of the palace.

'May we see the Queen?' asked Karen's mother timidly.

The footman couldn't wait to let them in. 'Her Majesty was absolutely distraught this morning. First she lost her jewel, and then she lost her pussy cat. She *will* be pleased to see Herbie safe and sound.'

Indeed she was. The Queen came running up the corridor and scooped Herbie into her arms. Into her private room they all marched and there was such a chatter as never was heard before inside the palace!

'Bring lots of cream cakes and honey wine,' ordered Her Majesty.

Eventually Karen's mother had to insist that they start on their return journey for Karen's father would be back home in the early evening. 'Goodbye, Herbie, maybe we'll meet again one day.'

Herbie contented himself with rubbing round their legs. He mustn't try out his voice just yet. At long last the Queen was on her own. Herbie snuggled close, then tried out his voice. What a funny squeak! He tried again; that was better. Her Majesty took no notice at first, then ... '*What* did you say, Herbie? Did I hear aright? The magic stone is right under the floorboards in my bedroom!'

Then the sudden realisation of it all came over her. She trembled with excitement. Her pussy could talk! Yet even as she thought this the magic was wearing off and Herbie found with relief that only a miaow came from him now. Golly, he didn't want to talk the rest of his life. Whatever would the other cats say?

Queen Esmeralda lost no time in ordering workmen to take up the floorboards. The mice family scattered in dismay when the noise started up above.

'I do believe that ghastly cat is back again,' glowered Milly Mouse.

'Shall we take the stone with us?' asked Marmaduke.

'No, it's too heavy. It will hold us up. We need to get out through the hole in the corridor before that awful cat pounces.'

So they did, and took up new quarters in the stables outside.

'My gorgeous gem,' cried Queen Esmeralda. 'Send for the Court jeweller. Tell him to fix it into my crown immediately. Here, I can't risk losing it again.'

Herbie sneaked off to see Tabby Topaz. 'What superb kittens, my dear. I have an excellent home for one of them. Ah, yes, this one is the image of me. I will call for him in three weeks' time!' Off he sped to his mistress and noted, with great approval, the red gem resplendent in its rightful place.

On the morning of the fair Karen was delighted to see Herbie approaching whilst they were picnicking. He had something in his mouth. Oh, a dear little kitten! He dropped it into her lap, and purred madly.

'See, Daddy, the pussy we told you about. He's brought me a lovely kitten. What shall I call it? Just call it Magic, did you say, Herbie? Do you know, Mummy, I imagined Herbie said that. Wasn't I silly?'

THE LAZY FAIRY

Candy was a lazy little fairy. She was always begging lifts from the dragonflies.

'Oh, please,' she would say, 'get me back to Fairyland before the emerald gates shut for the night. Dear dragonfly, your wings beat so much faster than mine, and really I'm so tired.' And here she would yawn so realistically that the dragonfly would take pity on her and tell the little fairy to hop aboard! He wasn't to know that Candy had been day-dreaming most of the evening instead of helping to close up the petals of the flowers for the night.

'My, but you *are* getting heavy,' said Desmond Dragonfly one evening. 'If you put on much more weight you will have to ask the birds to give you a ride!' Candy wasn't very pleased about this for she didn't really care for the feathers – they made her sneeze!

One evening Candy suddenly noticed that all the other fairies had gone from the lovely field where they had been flitting about, closing the daisy petals for the night. 'Good gracious me, I really have left it late tonight!' she exclaimed and looked around for her friend, Desmond Dragonfly.

Frantically she flitted from buttercup to daisy and she began to fear that he too was settling down for a

good night's sleep.

'Oh, Desmond, there you are! I'm really on the last minute tonight and the Fairy Queen says that the emerald gates will be closed promptly from now onwards. She has noticed that I'm always the last one in.'

'You are the limit,' grumbled Desmond. 'I'd promised myself an early night too. I've got a heavy day tomorrow – our annual gathering is taking place in Oak Woods. I suppose I can do the journey for you just this once more.'

'Oh, thank you,' breathed Candy demurely.

Quickly she hopped on and settled herself comfortably for the ride. His wings were simply superb – so beautiful and strong. In no time at all they arrived at the emerald gates, and, wonder of wonders, they were still wide open.

'Thank you, dear Dragonfly,' she trilled happily and jumped off in the twinkle of an eye.

'That's the last time, you know,' chided Desmond. 'Stop being so lazy. I bet you haven't used your wings properly for simply ages. Look well if they start losing their strength!'

Candy wasn't a bit bothered. She snuggled down for the night in her little mushroom home and dreamed of all the nice things she planned to do on the morrow.

She woke to a bright, sunny day, and having breakfasted on honey and toast, she made her way to the emerald gates.

'Candy,' called one fairy, 'you are wanted in the sorting glen today!'

'Bother!' muttered Candy. She didn't care for sorting all the berries in different piles. However, she knew better than to disobey so, reluctantly, she joined the other fairies as they busied themselves among the crimson and orange berries.

'You *are* getting fat, Candy,' said Fairy Primrose, gleefully. 'Your wings won't bear your weight before long!'

'It's all this taxi-ing about on Desmond Dragonfly,' chuckled another.

'Yes, and all this day-dreaming, instead of doing some work,' said Fairy Jasmine.

'You're only jealous because Desmond and I get on so well,' glowered Candy. 'I'm going, I've done my share.'

Off she sped towards her lovely hideaway – a mossy couch of green velvet. Oh, how comfortable it was! The day was promising to be rather too hot for her liking. Thank goodness she had found a spot in the shade. Soon the warmth of the sun and the murmuring of the insects lulled her to sleep. On she slept through the sunny hours and woke to find herself just a little chilly.

'My, how tired I must have been,' she yawned. 'I'm so hungry too – I must have missed tea. Thank goodness I brought some berries with me from the sorting glen.' And she nibbled away contentedly.

She finished off with a lovely long drink from the little stream nearby. She had never followed it to see where it meandered – it had always been far too much trouble but, today, she was curious to see round the next bend. She paused here and there to admire the pretty, wild flowers of pink and mauve, the like of which she had never seen before in the fields. So engrossed was she that she did not notice the shadows lengthen, until Reginald Rabbit, hopping by, scolded, 'You'll be locked out of Fairyland tonight and no mistake, Fairy Candy!'

'Not to worry,' said Candy, airily, 'Desmond Dragonfly will give me a lift, I'm sure – he always does.'

'Oh, indeed,' chuckled Reginald, 'I believe he's staying at a friend's tonight, over at Oak Woods.'

Candy's face fell. Oh, dear, she'd forgotten all about that. He had warned her.

'Never mind, I'll just have to hurry up and make my wings beat faster than usual.' And the little fairy waved her rainbow wings gently, preparing to take off. But, horror of horrors! There was simply no power in them at all. She ran along the ground with wings outstretched, but no! They were too weak and wouldn't lift her even one inch off the ground.

'Aha!' exclaimed Reginald with a disapproving air. 'You're too fat and, as you haven't been exercising your wings for such a long time, they won't take the strain. We've all been expecting such a thing to happen for a while – *now* it has!'

Candy began to cry. Then she had a bright idea. 'Couldn't you take me on your back, dear Mr Reginald?'

'Well, I'd like to lend a helping hand, but, you see, I need to return to my wife and children. Mopsy is poorly and I have just been for some medicine for her from the Wizard. There simply isn't enough time. The emerald gates will be shut by the time I reach our burrow to give her the first dose. It's so important there's no delay in giving the first spoonful. I tell you what, though, I'll put you up for the night. It might be a little rough, you're used to such comfort in Fairyland – but you're very welcome!'

He led the way to his little burrow. Mrs Rabbit wasn't a bit pleased to see Candy. She had enough to do looking after her family and Mopsy, without having a guest – and a fat one at that! Down the rabbit hole popped Reginald, with Candy a close second.

'This is the bedtime burrow,' he gestured proudly.

It was worse than Candy had expected. No velvet couches, just earth with a few leaves strewn around. Moreover it was crowded! Six tiny bunnies peeped out and, recognising her, giggled helplessly. Shame-facedly, Candy lay down at the farthest end of the burrow and pretended to fall asleep so that they wouldn't know she had heard their comments:

'Oh, what *will* the Fairy Queen say!'

'Isn't she the fattest fairy you ever did see?'

All the same, she did fall asleep at long last and woke to find Mrs Rabbit standing over her, saying, 'I'm sorry, but you'll have to get up now. I need to sweep out the burrow. But here are some nice berries for breakfast. Eat them in the dining burrow.'

'Thank you so much,' smiled Candy. Really, the Rabbit Family had been so good to her. It would have been so uncomfortable out in the woods all night. Who knows – an awful dog or pussy might have found her!

The little fairy decided she had had a lucky escape; all she needed to do now was to take her leave of the bunnies and slowly walk back to Fairyland. Perhaps the Fairy Queen wouldn't be too cross after all, and she would exercise her wings religiously every single day till they were as good as new. Maybe Mrs Rabbit would like some help with the breakfast pots?

Gathering up her acorn cup and tiny wooden plate, she went back to the bedtime burrow. What a commotion! Just what was going on? All the little bunnies were squeaking at once and, there on the floor, was the precious medicine, running in a brown stream, everywhere!

'Popsy pushed me, Mother,' quivered a sweet little bit of fluff.

'That I didn't,' stoutly denied her brother.

Mrs Rabbit was in a state. 'Whatever are we going to do? Your father isn't a bit well this morning. We must get another bottle of medicine from the Wizard, but I can't go all that way myself and leave you bunnies and poor Father alone.'

Fairy Candy was upset. She knew what was expected of her, but what a long time it was going to take her without the assistance of her wings! The Wizard lived right on top of a craggy rock, goodness knows how many fairy miles from here. The Fairy Queen was certainly going to be very cross if she spent two whole nights out of Fairyland. What a thought – she might even banish her for ever!

Timidly she ventured, 'Maybe I could go for your medicine?'

'What a simply splendid idea!' they all chorused.

Mrs Rabbit bustled about in charge of things once more. 'Now, do take this haversack and, see – I've put lots of soft leaves inside to protect the bottle. Take these berries too in case you get hungry along the way.'

All the bunnies, save Mopsy, came to see her off. Such kind little bunnies now! 'You know,' said one, 'I do believe Fairy Candy is a good, kind-hearted fairy.'

'Let me point the way,' shouted another. 'You can't miss the rock.'

There, towering above the trees was a huge, brown rock and perched on top something shining like silver in the sunlight. Candy's heart missed a beat; she'd no idea she had to climb so far. Still, she was the only one they could rely on – the bunnies were much too young for such an adventure. Somehow she felt better and a little proud of herself.

'Bye,' she called out and, picking her way carefully among the tree roots, she set out.

She made good progress through the wood, grateful for the shade, and was tempted to partake of some of the berries. Oh, to sit beneath the shade of a beautiful oak tree – but just suppose she fell asleep again! She hurried on, wishing with all her heart that she could fly, as every fairy was meant to do.

There was the rock, towering above her. She made sure that her haversack was firmly fastened about her shoulders and began the climb, snatching at tufts of grass growing in the clefts. Oh, how she panted, slithering up the steep slopes! How she wished she was nice and slim!

The birds were frankly amazed to see a little fairy puffing up the hill. 'Use your wings, you stupid fairy,' twittered one.

'Trying to slim?' croaked another.

Candy hadn't enough breath to retort, she just kept going. With one last great heave, she pulled herself up and onto the clifftop. Gratefully she sank down on the mossy grass and surveyed the scene below. What a gorgeous view! There in the distance shone the lovely, emerald gates of Fairyland. She felt a bit homesick. Would anyone really miss her? Or did they think – well, she never did much work anyway. No use feeling sorry for herself. Now to seek out the Wizard. What if he was away from home today? Tentatively she flexed her wings and tried a little run across the courtyard. Yes, they were definitely better. Perhaps she had lost a bit of weight during her adventure?

Woody the Elf answered to her knock on the great oak door and he seemed quite concerned to see Fairy

Candy looking so hot and tired.

'Come this way and partake of a sweet cup of nectar,' he offered.

'Oh, thank you, Woody, that would be lovely, but I mustn't linger because I must get Mopsy's medicine to her before she gets worse.'

'That's a good fairy,' boomed a deep voice and, appearing like magic behind her, stood the Wizard! He didn't seem a bit surprised to see Candy and he had quite a twinkle in his eye.

'I'll get you the medicine right away,' he promised.

Clutching the precious medicine, the little fairy sped to the door. She was embarrassed. Did the Wizard know about her wings? Still – he looked so kind. She paused at the door. 'Oh, Mr Wizard, I am so worried about my wings. They are a little better, but do you think they will ever be fully recovered?'

'I think they already are,' he said, gravely. 'Exercise of any sort is good for them but better still are good deeds. Fairies, you know, need to do at least one good deed every day to keep their wings in tip-top condition!'

Candy couldn't wait to try them. With a fervent 'Thank you,' she really twinkled out of his presence and out of the door, soaring high in the air without the least bit of effort. The Rabbit Family was astonished to see her back so early.

'What a helpful fairy you are! Do come and see us sometime won't you, and we can play some lovely games together.'

Mr Rabbit was sure he would soon be much better when he had had some of the Wizard's medicine.

'I must get back to Fairyland immediately,' worried Candy. 'I need to make my apologies.'

With many goodbyes, they waved her off, admiring

the ease with which she gaily dipped and swirled high in the air. Yes, everyone had missed Candy. The Fairy Queen was rather stern at first, but she softened when she heard all about the little fairy's adventures.

'I do believe you are slimmer,' said Fairy Primrose, kindly.

'Desmond Dragonfly has been in to enquire about you,' whispered Fairy Jasmine.

Candy was a little sad; she would miss flying aboard Desmond. Well, perhaps once in a way – her Birthday! Yes, that was it! She would invite all the dragonflies to a super birthday tea and afterwards the fairies could have rides round Fairyland. What a lovely idea. She must start planning at once. But first she must hurry off with the rest and put the daisies and buttercups to sleep.

THE RAINBOW-COLOURED BALL

Higher and higher spun the rainbow-coloured ball. The little girl was delighted with it. Really it was yellow with blue and red spots, but when it was moving it was a wonderful colour. Again and again Pamela caught and threw her ball till, one time, she missed and over the garden fence it went and out into the field beyond. Quickly she climbed the fence and chased it as it bowled along into the soft, green meadow.

'Goodness me,' she panted, 'what a long way you're going!'

'Aha,' replied the ball, 'you can't catch me, just you see!'

Pamela was so astonished at hearing this that she nearly tripped over a clump of dandelions!

'Well, you're certainly not going to get away from me – you're my lovely new ball.' And she sprinted off with renewed energy.

Down the meadow they ran till they came to a little brook and here the ball made a sharp turn and bumped alongside till they came to a little stone bridge.

Seeing that Pamela was catching up and would certainly pick him up soon, the ball sighed and said, 'All right then, as a special treat I'll let you come with me.'

'Why, where are you off to?' demanded Pamela, 'and why are we stopping here?'

'One question at a time please,' grunted the ball. 'First we have to get you a decent size or you'll frighten the others away. Now you see this red spot on me, the biggest one? Well, press it three times and say, 'I want to be three times as small.'

Pamela didn't know whether to do it or to go home to her lovely safe garden but, at last, with a brave air, she pressed the spot and, lo and behold, she was small already. The ball bumped against a square stone under the bridge and the bridge swung open, revealing a narrow passage lit by a lot of tiny fairy lights. Down this they hurried and at last they came out by the side of a field.

Pamela stared and stared at what she saw. Hundreds and hundreds of balls were rolling and bowling in from all directions. Little ones. Big ones. Dirty ones. Clean ones. Beautiful ones and, frankly, ugly ones.

'This,' said her rainbow ball, 'is the yearly gathering of all the balls. You see that gorgeous ball over there? He is the King of all the balls. He has come a long way and he is the property of the Princess Suzanne of Switzerland.'

Here and there were stalls and, for one minute, Pamela thought she had come to the fair! At one stall elves, clad in green aprons, were busy stitching up all the torn balls. At another elves, in red aprons, were painting the faded ones. And at yet another elves, clad in yellow overalls, were giving the dirty balls a bath! It was to the bathing stall that Pamela and her rainbow ball hurried.

'Come along and help,' he chuckled, 'don't forget your yellow overall!'

The little girl found herself dipping and scrubbing hundreds and hundreds of black and grey balls. How rewarding to see pretty colours revealed and to hear the squeaks of thanks! At long last the queue had gone, and it was time for refreshments. Elves in blue aprons brought nectar drinks and some delicious cakes, the like of which Pamela had never tasted before. The balls were very polite to her and, every now and again she would ask to bounce an extra nice-looking one when it took her fancy. It was hard to choose for now the balls were in very good shape and she wondered just what their owners would say when they returned home.

'Quiet for the King!' shouted a pompous-looking purple ball.

Everyone rolled still and the golden ball floated gently into the branch of a tree so that everyone could see him better. He said that he was glad to see them all looking so well turned-out, and 'three cheers' for the elves and for Miss Pamela.

Pamela grew quite pink with pleasure! After the cheers had subsided the King announced that he would look into any complaints the balls had against their owners. He himself was still very happy with the Princess, but he would have to go soon, for she would be missing him and that would make her very unhappy.

One or two balls went to the foot of the tree to ask for advice and, after this was given, the King floated up and up into the blue sky till they could see him no more. 'My word, I didn't know that balls could really fly!' exclaimed Pamela.

'Well, he is very special,' said her ball, proudly. 'He will have a long journey over the mountains and sea till he reaches the palace.'

All the other balls were saying their goodbyes and rolling and bowling away from all corners of the field. Some were going their way, and Pamela recognised balls owned by her little friends in the avenue. All too soon they came out of the little passage and it was time for Pamela to become her normal size again. So she pressed the red spot again and chanted, 'I want to be three times as big.'

To her great relief she was – she had been a bit worried about getting back to her own size! On the way home Pamela bounced and threw her lovely rainbow ball. They had never had such a delightful time, because just for a while the ball could talk back to her. Now they had reached her garden fence and he could no longer speak.

'Maybe next year he'll take me again,' she thought and ran gaily inside to tell her mother all about it.

THE PINK DEWDROP

Fairy Crystal had been naughty. Yes, really naughty. She had taken a bar of delicious fairy nougat which did not belong to her. The Fairy Queen was most upset.

'Whatever came over you to do such a thing?' she admonished.

The fairy hung her head and blushed.

'This is a very serious matter indeed,' scolded the Queen. 'I must banish you from Fairyland and you must not return until you have brought me a pink dewdrop.'

'A pink dewdrop!' echoed Fairy Crystal. 'I have never seen such a dewdrop – I shall never be able to return to Fairyland.'

Slowly she flew through the lovely silver gates of Fairyland and the other fairies watched her go. Some were very sorry to see their friend banished, but others thought she had been rightly punished.

'Whatever came over me to take the nougat bar?' moaned the little fairy. 'I knew it must have dropped from someone's pocket; I should have returned it to the lost property room. But it's no use crying now. Somehow I must find the pink dewdrop and then I will be able to return to Fairyland, and then I must be a very good little fairy for ever more.'

Thus thinking, she flew into a deep green forest and looked about for someone to talk with. The rabbits popped up and said, 'Good gracious me! Look who's here – Fairy Crystal! Have you come to gather berries?'

The fairy looked sad. 'I've been a bad fairy and no-one wants me in Fairyland until I bring back a pink dewdrop, though how that will make me a better fairy I do not know!'

'Hm,' said Mother Rabbit, 'that is a problem, but whilst you're here, will you be good to us and see if you can bring me a little carrot for Reggie? He has been poorly and now he says a little carrot would just set him right again.'

'Of course I will,' said Fairy Crystal and she flew away out of the wood in the direction of a farm where she knew she might find a juicy carrot.

Dolly and Dickie Donkey were enjoying a lovely meal of them. They looked up from their dinner. 'Why it's Fairy Crystal. Like a small juicy carrot?'

'That's just what I fancy right now.'

Dickie nudged a small, sweet carrot in her direction. 'Any news Fairy Crystal?'

She hung her head. 'I'm the only news – I have to keep out of Fairyland until I find a pink dewdrop. You see I ate a nougat bar which belonged to someone else.'

'Oh, dear!' brayed Dolly. 'Still, I bet it was tempting. Can't say I blame you!'

'A pink dewdrop you say!' exclaimed Dickie. 'What an extraordinary thing! Say, how about taking one at dawn? Would that do?'

'I doubt it,' quavered Crystal, 'the pink glow would leave it as soon as I entered the palace.'

'Sorry we can't help you.' The donkeys returned to

their munching.

Fairy Crystal flew off to give her tonic to Reggie Rabbit. His little eyes were bright with anticipation. 'Ooh, thank you little fairy; I feel better already.'

He crunched the orange delicacy happily.

Mrs Rabbit looked fondly at her son. 'I'll ask around about that pink dewdrop. I've been thinking – could you prick your finger, Fairy Crystal?'

The little fairy considered this idea seriously. 'I think I had better not cheat the Fairy Queen. That would never do! Bye, Mrs Rabbit, I must be on my way.'

She flew out of the forest, past the farm and on to the hills. Ah, there was the dear old scarecrow. She settled on his shoulder.

'How are you dear Mr Turnip?'

'Oh, fair enough,' came the crackling reply. 'Still get the birds nesting in my pockets. Company, you know, seeing as I don't get around much! Birds are such gossips! Anything I can do for you Fairy Crystal? How are you getting along in Fairyland?'

The little fairy told him her weary story.

'You've come to just the right person. I know where you can get a pink dewdrop.'

'Oh, you really do, how wonderful!'

'Yes, my dear, I've not forgotten the way you mended my poor old straw face for me. Nice bit of magic you have in that wand. How come you can't wish up a pink dewdrop?'

'Didn't you know, Mr Turnip, fairies can't use their magic to help them out of a scrape?'

'Fancy that! Is that so? Now about that dewdrop. You must fly on over the hills. Over the other side is lovely country and you'll see a pink cottage shaped just like a beehive. Can't miss it! In the garden grow

85

lovely poppies and the pink ones are said to be very special. They can do all manner of wonderful things provided you know how to use them! Early in the morning you'll find pink dewdrops in their hearts!'

Fairy Crystal clapped her hands. 'How marvellous!' Then a thought struck her. 'But whose garden is it, Mr Turnip?'

'Why, the Poppy Sisters live there. Depends if they like the look of you, really. They're very mysterious.'

'Ooh, I do hope so,' she cried, spreading her wings.

'Just a minute,' shouted Mr Turnip. 'How are you going to carry it back to Fairyland?'

Fairy Crystal looked surprised. 'I thought I'd take the flower as well.'

'Bit risky,' crackled he, 'supposing the Poppy Sisters won't allow you? If I were you I'd fly to the beach and pick one of the periwinkle shells.

'What a super idea, Mr Turnip! Thank you, thank you!'

She darted off. Halfway there she had to descend and eat some berries. She was faint with hunger. Sitting on a fallen tree trunk, she smiled with relief.

Sunny Squirrel looked down from his tree. 'Hi, Fairy Crystal, nice to see you.'

The little fairy told him of her quest. He pondered. 'Yes, looks as if you'll soon have a pink dewdrop. Still, nothing like being sure. I happen to know the Poppy Sisters are very partial to walnuts. If you like I can give you one or two. Not forgotten how you saved my tail from the nasty trap!' He scurried away and returned with some fat, juicy walnuts which she packed into her haversack.

'Bye, Sunny Squirrel.'

'Good luck!' he called.

Soon she was hovering over the beach and scanning the shells for a periwinkle just the right size. Ah, there looked a likely specimen. She alighted and popped the periwinkle in her haversack. Oh, she was tired! She flopped down on a rock and gave a deep sigh. Sammy Seagull spotted her as he swooped and whizzed over the water's edge.

'Hi, Fairy Crystal, how come you're so far away from Fairyland today? I thought today was a special party day?'

He settled down beside her and listened to her weary story.

'Come now, it's not too bad – things will sort themselves out, I'm sure. The thing to do is to be nice and strong for your venture!'

He looked at her critically. 'All this diet of berries and fruit! Pah! What you need is a bit of protein!'

Off he flew and eventually came back with some lovely, fat shrimps. Fairy Crystal tucked into them and felt decidedly better. 'Come now,' he ordered. 'Climb on my back. I'll have you in the poppy garden in no time!'

How delightful it was to soar effortlessly over the countryside! A splash of colour lit up the land. 'There it is, little fairy!'

'Oh, what a gorgeous garden!' Her eyes shone with pleasure and excitement.

'Yes, it's the best for miles around.'

Lots of beautiful poppies nodded and swayed in the gentle breeze. Exotic reds, flaming pinks, pure whites and sunshine yellows.

'So here I find the pink dewdrop.'

Fairy Crystal gazed at a clump of pink poppies. She

would need to wait till the following morning. Sammy Seagull considered. 'Now you're on your own, little fairy. Go and find the Poppy Sisters. I'm sure they'll be sympathetic. They'll let you stay with them for the night! I'll wait here by the fence. Come to me if you're in trouble. I've not forgotten how you cleaned the oil from my feathers last year!'

She slid from his back and floated up the path towards the little green door. Timidly she knocked. What kind of people were the Poppy Sisters? They were not pixies nor fairies. Her thoughts were interrupted. The door was opening. Two wee folk stood there; two sisters with bright red, flowing hair. Fairy Crystal suppressed a smile They were so thin, they reminded her very much of two bright red poppies!

'Why, we have a fairy come to visit us, sister Milly!'

'Indeed we have, sister Dilly! Come along in.'

The little fairy was delighted.

'Have a cup of our special tea, do!' Fairy Crystal relaxed with relief. Now to tell her story, but first she must offer her present – the lovely walnuts. As they nibbled away she described in detail the events of the day. 'And so,' faltered the little fairy, 'if you would let me stay with you till dawn, then I must collect the pink dewdrop.'

Milly looked at Dilly. 'Shall we consult our little book, dear? We won't be long. Just make yourself comfortable.'

Fairy Crystal was a bit alarmed. What was the mystery about the dewdrop?'

Milly and Dilly looked at each other. 'I fancy there's some sort of magic about our pink poppies. Wasn't there some recipe in our little black book Mother left us?'

Excitedly they pored over the pages. 'Here it is,' cried Dilly. 'Pink dewdrop!' As they read, their eyes widened with astonishment. 'Fancy that!' they chorused. 'Oh, but I don't think we had better tell that to a little fairy!'

'No better not!'

Spritely they entered the sitting room. 'Of course you may stay the night dear Fairy Crystal. We'll prepare your room right away!'

'I'll just run and tell Sammy Seagull I'm all right,' said the little fairy thankfully.

She spent a very comfortable night, and was fresh as a daisy to meet the coming day. The sisters seemed as excited as she and all three had a quick and light breakfast. Fairy Crystal washed out the periwinkle carefully, and they all trooped out into the garden to claim a pink dewdrop.

The birds were frankly amazed as the little procession wended its way through the garden to the clump of pink poppies. Susie Sparrow nearly fell out of her nest watching the sisters help Fairy Crystal tilt the poppy till the precious liquid ran into the shell. 'Guess what I've just seen,' she trilled.

'Oh, go back to sleep,' croaked Stevie.

'Wait till I tell Jenny Wren tomorrow,' thought Susie, hugging this little secret to herself.

With grateful goodbyes Fairy Crystal was on her way. Her mission nearly accomplished, she was full of energy. She entered the gates of Fairyland just as everyone was starting work.

'Nice to see you back,' shouted the gatekeeper. 'We've all missed you!'

She flew up to the palace door. 'May I see the Queen?'

'Just wait inside,' ordered a fat green elf, majestically.

Fairy Crystal sat on a red velvet chair clutching her periwinkle. A door opened. The Queen herself hurried forward.

'Oh, you are back so soon, Fairy Crystal. Have you come to apologise again? I suppose you know by now there isn't any such thing as a pink dewdrop! But what is this you are giving me? A periwinkle!' She laughed.

'Careful, Your Majesty, it contains a pink dewdrop!'

The Queen's face lit up. 'Oh, how wonderful, so my little black book was right!'

She tenderly took the periwinkle and tilted its contents into her mouth.

'Thank you Fairy Crystal, you don't know how grateful I am! Go back to your normal duties. We will say no more about the nougat bar.'

The little fairy flew off to her toadstool house. She sighed. 'All that fuss over a pink dewdrop.' Ah, well, she supposed the venture had made her appreciative of living in Fairyland. Just imagine, the Queen was so excited about a pink dewdrop – she had forgotten to ask where it came from! Fairy Crystal often puzzled over the pink dewdrop. What a mystery it was!

One day the Queen summoned her to the Palace. 'Dear Fairy Crystal you shall be the very first to know our secret. Soon the King and I will have our longed-for baby! The pink dewdrop helped make this possible because of its magical properties!'

Fairy Crystal clapped her hands with delight. She could hardly wait for the birth of the baby. Would it be a Princess? Indeed it was, and I will leave you to guess her name!

MIRANDA'S RAINBOW

Miranda was six years old that very day and one of her birthday presents was a pair of lovely, shiny red, wellington boots. Oh, the joy of pirouetting in front of the long, wardrobe mirror to admire her gloriously shod feet! Anxiously she scanned the sky. Not a cloud in sight! It certainly looked as if rain was not the order of the day.

Normally, like any other little girl, Miranda would have rejoiced at the prospect of a sunny day for her birthday party, which was to be held outdoors in their huge, rambling garden. Lots of little wooden tables had already been erected and white-painted chairs clustered about. Posies of marigolds and marguerites centred each table to match the beflowered plates and napkins. Tea was at four o'clock, but it was only one o'clock. Miranda had partaken of a light lunch, and it was much too early to dress in the pretty, blue-smocked frock specially bought for the occasion. Mother was very busy scurrying between kitchen and pantry, concocting lots of delicious goodies for the feast.

Miranda pondered. What could she do to while away the hours? Ah, how about picking some daisies and buttercups in the field at the end of the garden? Maybe one or two red clover could be found – she did so love their scent. She peeped over the fence. The grass was high and damp with the rain of the last few days. What a marvellous excuse to wear her new wellies!

She dashed happily up the stairs and lovingly opened the shoe box. Quickly she drew on the shiny boots and flew downstairs. She popped her head round the kitchen door, breathlessly saying, 'I'm picking buttercups and daisies, Mummy.'

Striding down the garden path, she was at least six inches taller! There was a convenient gap between the fence posts, and Miranda was expert at squeezing through. She carefully made her way round the grass edge and by the hedge, so she wouldn't flatten the tall, thick grass. Nearby was a secret little dell – sometimes she could find the very best daisies here, lovely and big and pink-tipped. She stopped short, holding her breath. How perfectly wonderful! Just what she had longed for on this special day – a dinky pool. She could try out her new boots right away. With a rapturous expression on her face Miranda stepped boldly in the shallow water, noting with satisfaction that the water came up to at least three inches over her feet. Someone had thrown away a chunk of orange peel and there it was idly floating this way and that, like a toy boat. She kicked it to the side where it continued to bob about till she firmly planted her foot on it.

Then – what was that? Incredibly a rainbow-hue emerged from under her red wellies. It seemed to be coming from the orange peel. Perhaps if she stamped on it again the same thing would happen. This time a lovely expanse of rainbow appeared on the surface of the pool, and it grew and grew till Miranda's eyes were dazzled with the glorious colours. Red, yellow, green and blue, indigo, violet and orange. Wonderingly she gazed at the orange peel – but surely it was now transformed into a sweet little boat, and someone was in it too! A beautiful fairy dressed in gorgeous rainbow hues! Fascinated, she watched the fairy sail right up to her and was even more amazed when a silvery voice asked her if she would like a trip to Rainbow Land. Miranda was only too willing, but couldn't see how she could possibly fit into the boat.

'No problem,' tinkled the fairy and she waved her diamond wand.

In no time at all the birthday girl was settled comfortably in the orange craft which skimmed smoothly over the water till they came to a bridge – a wonderful bridge just like a rainbow. The fairy held Miranda's hand tightly and led her up some steps and the steep arc of the rainbow. What a wonderful view they had! The daisies and buttercups were like upturned umbrellas and lots of ants, flies and grasshoppers were scurrying to and fro just like humanfolk.

'We must hurry,' said Fairy Rainbow, 'we only have a short time. We must let you see our lovely land, but return before the rainbow fades. Let's run now, we're slipping down the other side.'

Miranda was dazzled at the glow of golden light emerging from the end of the rainbow. What a beautiful land it must be! Silvery laughter could be heard and, yes, there were lots of little fairies dressed all in blue, or red, or yellow, or indigo, or green, or violet or orange.

'A visitor, how delightful,' said Fairy Bluebow, 'is she coming to dance with us at our Anniversary Ball?'

95

'My what perfectly lovely boots she has on her feet,' trilled Fairy Violet.

'Yes,' smiled Fairy Rainbow, 'they helped to make the special magic for her visit to Rainbow Land. And, of course, it is her birthday too!'

Laughingly they put their arms about the little girl and guided her to a velvety-green lawn where myriads of fairies were already dancing away to the music provided by the harebells and bluebells. Miranda's wellingtons were light as air as she twirled this way and that, revelling in the sight of the rainbow-hued dancers enjoying their festive ball in honour of Midsummer's Day.

Breathlessly she sank down on one of the comfy toadstools and was happy to accept an acorn cup, full of nectar, offered by a beaming elf-waiter. The music began again and Miranda's feet itched to be away and to join in the merry throng, but Fairy Rainbow was by her side, whispering that, alas, the rainbow was fading, and they must hurry back.

Reluctantly the little girl waved goodbye to her fairy friends and began the long journey back, up the steep arc of the rainbow.

'Hurry,' chided Fairy Rainbow, 'here, catch hold of my wand, and I will pull you.'

'But the rainbow is as bright as ever,' complained Miranda.

'Yes, this side is, but when we reach the top we may not be able to see our way clearly,' worried the little fairy.

Sure enough the road ahead became misty and Miranda was so glad she had hold of the wand.

'I dare not come any further with you, but if I seat you on this little magic rose leaf, and give you a push, I think you will land safe and sound in your special dell.'

96

With these words, Fairy Rainbow took the leaf carefully from her knapsack and settled Miranda firmly on it. 'Bye,' she called, 'come and see us again when you are seven years old.' And the little girl slid slowly and smoothly through the misty air.

With a swish and a plop she was by the side of the pool which really looked enormous.

'Oh, dear! She forgot to wave her wand over me,' gasped Miranda and alighted from her rose leaf. But, wonder of wonders, the minute she arose, the pool grew smaller and smaller and in amazement she watched the leaf waft up and up till it was out of sight. It surely was on its way back to Rainbow Land.

'What a wonderful birthday treat I had,' chuckled Miranda. 'Now where is the magic orange peel?'

But do you know it had vanished! 'I really must remember to take an orange to the dell next year,' she said to herself.

LITTLE RED LADYBIRD

Jenny-May was thrilled to bits! She had on a brand new cardigan. A lovely red one with the sweetest little ladybird buttons. Today she was going to her best friend's party. Jenny had wriggled impatiently whilst Mother had ironed her party dress of white muslin, sprigged with tiny, red flowers. At last it was ready and she quickly drew it over her head and let Mother tie the sash of red, velvet ribbon.

'I think you had better have a cardigan for the wind is chilly today,' said Mother.

'Oh, no!' moaned Jenny-May. 'Not that lumpy white one!'

'Just you wait and see,' smiled Mother. 'I have bought you a lovely new one for your birthday next month, but I guess you can wear it today. Do look after it, though, and don't lose any buttons, because they are so very special!'

What a pretty cardigan she carried over her arm!

'See, there are six little ladybird buttons with gilt spots. I do believe there is an extra one sewn on underneath in case one does get lost. Where I would get buttons like that I'm sure I don't know.'

'Oh, I'll be very careful, Mother,' cried Jenny-May. 'Don't you worry,' and off she danced to look at her

reflection in the mirror.

'It's much too soon to go to Betty's party,' said Mother. 'Now just you go and read a book in the summer-house until it's time to go.'

So off skipped Jenny-May into the garden. However, after reading one of her favourite animal stories, she grew bored. She was really much too excited to sit still for very long, so she danced onto the lawn and went round and round till she was dizzy. Pausing for breath, she stooped and smelled the fragrance from the lovely pink roses, not noticing that a wayward branch had caught hold so very gently but firmly, of her cardigan!

What was that? Horror of horrors, her new possession was in the hands of a prickly rose stem! She carefully tried to unwind the branch and thought she had succeeded without damage to her cardigan, but then, with great surprise, she saw one of her little ladybird buttons suddenly become air-borne.

There was a tiny fairy hanging onto the button and nearly succeeding in carrying it away. Jenny-May shot out her hand and grasped them both very securely.

'Oh,' squealed the fairy. 'Let go!'

'That's *my* button,' panted Jenny-May, 'my very special button!'

The fairy looked down at the cardigan. 'You have enough buttons,' she pouted. 'Couldn't you spare just this one?'

Jenny-May looked and, to be sure, she had all her buttons. Ah, but what about the spare one? Yes, the fairy had that one clutched to her body. 'If you don't let me have this one,' she said, 'I won't win the prize for the best collection.'

'Collection of what?' enquired Jenny-May.

101

'Why, buttons, of course!'

The little fairy looked very woebegone, and began to cry. 'My w-wand is getting very old and – I do n-need a new one. S-see it is all b-bent, and my magic doesn't always work. The prize is a l-lovely new one, guaranteed to do the most up-to-date spells.'

Jenny-May was a kind-hearted little girl and didn't know what to do about this new development. 'I wish I could let you have it, but supposing I need it if I lose another button? Mother will be very cross.'

'I know,' said the fairy, brightening up. 'I'll take you with me to Fairyland!'

'To Fairyland,' echoed Jenny-May.

'Yes, come with me to our workshop where the elves will sew on your other buttons with magic thread, so they will never, ever come off. Then you can visit our special Museum containing all our unusual buttons. Oh, it will be fun!'

'But, I have to go to Betty's party in half-an-hour,' said Jenny-May worriedly.

'That's all right, we shall be there and back before then because our time isn't a bit like yours in Humanland. Half-an-hour is as good as three hours in Fairyland.'

'Fancy that!' exclaimed Jenny-May. 'In that case I will come with you. Which way is it?'

'Why, right here,' smiled the fairy, and she parted a rose petal, and slid right down into the centre of the rose. 'Oh, I forgot, you're a little bit on the large side,' she chuckled. 'Let me wave my magic wand to make you a better size!'

So she did but, it was quite true, the wand was old, and Jenny-May didn't get to be the right size until the fairy had waved it ten times!

'Follow me,' she said, at last, and she led the way

through layers and layers of sweet-smelling rose petals. At the heart of the rose she stopped and pressed lightly on the golden centre. A little door opened and led into a long green tunnel. They hurried along, taking turns to carry the ladybird button. As they came to the end lots and lots of fairies could be seen peeping in to see who was arriving with such an unusual companion.

'Why,' cried one, 'what a special button you have there Fairy Moss-Rose.'

'Introduce us to your friend,' begged the others.

'This is Jenny-May, and she is so kind. She has given me her lovely button, so I may hope to win the new wand.'

And the little fairy hopped up and down with excitement. 'Help me carry it to the Museum.'

So off they all went, admiring the ladybird's golden yellow spots and its red shiny coat.

The Museum was in a beautiful park. Lovely flower-beds were edged round with silver arches and lots of pretty toadstools shone in the sun. Something about them seemed vaguely familiar to Jenny-May. Fairy Moss-Rose triumphantly entered the Museum hall and brought her latest find to the elf-in-charge.

'How splendid,' said Elf Greenleaf. 'I think that makes you the winner, but, of course, we shall have to wait until the Fairy Queen comes to do the judging. Would you like to take your friend and show her all our prize buttons?'

So Jenny-May was led through the hall and taken to the display room where just hundreds and hundreds of unusual buttons were displayed in glass cases.

'These are very special,' whispered Fairy Moss-Rose, 'but your ladybird button will have pride of place, I'm sure.'

'However do you come by these?' asked Jenny-May.

'Oh, it's amazing how many people in Humanland lose hooks and eyes, and buttons and beads,' said her little fairy. 'Did you see the little "eyes" bordering the flower-beds? And the lovely big buttons for toadstool seats? You would be amazed if you could see everything we make with your buttons! We needed lots and lots of pearl buttons to renew the Museum roof. That is why we had this competition. I collected lots and lots, but I had to have a really special button for the Museum collection to qualify for the prize..'

Suddenly there was a stir and a murmuring. In swept the most gorgeous fairy you ever did see. She was clothed in silver and had the most beautiful, golden hair and bright, blue eyes. From all the rooms bordering the hall flew little fairies. They perched on the bannisters, on the steps and on the little toadstool seats.

Jenny-May became a bit bothered. Just supposing the Queen spoke to her? How would she dare to speak? Sure enough, the Queen of the Fairies came walking right up to her, but looked at Jenny-May with such a merry twinkle in her eyes that she was no longer nervous.

'Thank you so much for being such an understanding little girl,' she said. 'I'm so glad that Fairy Moss-Rose will now be able to have the coveted new wand. To tell the truth, she's been getting into quite some mix-ups with her wand! Your ladybird button is wonderful – we shall make a crystal case for it, and underneath we shall write how Fairy Moss-Rose came by it, and to whom it belonged.'

Once more Jenny-May was thrilled to bits. Fancy

being in the Hall of Fame in Fairyland!

'However,' continued the Queen, 'I'm sure you will be anxious to have all your other buttons sewn on with magic thread. So I will take you myself to the workshop.'

She just waved her wand and in a moment they were in a long green room where lots and lots of elves were busily mending fairy wings and stitching new buttons on fairy shoes!

One tiny elf, clad in buttercup-yellow, took Jenny-May's cardigan very carefully and laid it on a little, wooden bench. There on a giant reel was the magic thread. It looked like spun gold and the sight of the little elf, pulling the strands tightly round each ladybird button, made her eyes dazzle. In no time at all the work was done and, with a bow, the elf returned the cardigan.

'Oh, thank you so much,' smiled Jenny-May.

All this time the Queen had been touring the workshop, looking at the latest repairs and giving advice when some job was proving more difficult than usual.

Now she flew back to Jenny-May's side and said with a smile, 'Your mother is looking out of her window for you. I think it's time you were off to Betty's party. There isn't time today for you to see our storerooms which are stacked to the ceiling with useful buttons.'

Jenny-May had nearly forgotten all about the party! Well who wouldn't, with a trip to Fairyland? What a day this was!

'Oh, I've had a simply marvellous time,' she breathed.

'We were all so happy to have you,' answered the Queen. 'Here is Fairy Moss-Rose to escort you back to Humanland, and this time I don't think she will have any trouble with her wand!'

Swiftly they sped down a rosy path leading to the green tunnel. All the fairies came to see them off, admiring the sparkling new wand, which Fairy Moss-Rose carried so importantly. This time Jenny-May was back to her normal size with just one flick of the wand!

'Thank you so much,' cried Jenny-May as she sped down the lawn towards the back door.

'And thank you too,' tinkled Fairy Moss-Rose.

Jenny-May's mother was a bit cross when she owned-up about losing the spare button. She was quite amazed when Jenny-May told her that she mustn't worry – all the others were sewn on with magic thread!

As for Jenny-May, she thoroughly enjoyed the party. She never told anyone about her adventure, for already it was fading as in a dream. She didn't see the Fairy Queen sprinkle her with forgetful dust, for, after all, Fairyland was now stocked up with buttons. They didn't want little girls supplying them with any more!

THE PRINCE AND
THE GREEN GODDESS

Wacky Witch was in a temper. She stamped up and down in her black cave in the deep, dark forest. Saucy, her cat, had long ago fled to a safe spot far away. *He* didn't want to be turned into a rat or a bat! Oh, dear me no, he would wait till Wacky had vented her anger on someone else! And - what was the trouble this time? The little people of Flowerland had been celebrating the birth of a new princess. They had had a gorgeous display of fireworks and - guess what - one of the rockets had knocked Wacky off her broomstick as she sailed by! Though Wacky wasn't hurt, for she landed in a tree - she was decidedly ruffled. She'd make them sorry! Now, what kind of spell could she concoct?

She stopped her stamping and crowed with satisfaction. Flowerland was so proud of its lovely woods and fields filled with exquisite flowers. She'd spoil all that! Quickly she poked the embers of the fire, and rushed outside to draw water from the well. When the fire was merry and bright she filled a pot with water and selected different herbs from the bunches hung around the walls. The lotion boiled and bubbled, whilst Wacky stirred it slowly with a

long, horn spoon. Clouds and clouds of vapour filled the cave, then billowed out and floated towards the heart of Flowerland. Wacky hopped on her broomstick and guided the cloud till it was over the Palace. Slowly it descended. 'What a surprise they'll all have tomorrow morning!' she cackled.

Saucy peered out of his cosy basket of leaves. Wacky was winging her way back home, singing happily. He sighed. Someone was going to have a bad time pretty soon, but it wasn't *his* turn, thank goodness! He sauntered into the cave.

'There you are, Saucy. Come and have a lovely supper. Who's a darling pussy, then!'

The Princess at the Palace woke early. Her baby daughter was wide awake. The Princess carried her to the window, rocking her gently to and fro. Princess Marguerite never tired of the wonderful view over the park, with its enchanting beds of flowers. She mustn't draw the curtains – she might waken the Prince – but she peeped through a chink. So startled was she, she threw back the curtains, wakening him.

'Whatever . . . ?' The Prince sat up then, seeing his little daughter, he relaxed. 'Oh, dear, I expect I'll have to get used to these early mornings!'

Princess Marguerite sat on the bed. 'Do look out and tell me what you see, dear husband.'

The Prince smiled; he was ready to indulge his wife in this whim of hers. 'Why lots and lots of flowers, lots . . . . His words died away. He gazed out at the awful scene. The sky was emerald green, the grass and trees were blue and the flowers were all black!

The door burst open. In dashed the King and Queen. 'Oh, have you seen the terrible thing that has happened to our land?'

The baby cried *and* the Princess *and* the Queen!

109

Soon people were arriving at the Palace; the shocking colour scheme had spread throughout the country!

'Whatever can we do!' wailed the Queen.

'I bet it's the work of that wicked witch,' groaned the Prince.

The wisest people in the land were invited to the Palace, but no-one could come up with any good idea. Supposing someone *did* approach Wacky? She would just turn them into a spider or something awful!

Prince Rupert was silent. Could *he* do anything? 'Father shall I journey to the Wishing Pool and ask the Green Goddess for her advice?'

'What an excellent idea!' smiled the King.

'Oh, *do* take care,' worried his mother. Suddenly her face lit up. 'Take with you the gems your godmother gave you. They cannot grant wishes, but surely they may help you on your way.'

She brought out three gorgeous gems from a casket, an emerald, a sapphire and a diamond.

Prince Rupert kissed his wife and family goodbye, and jumped on his handsome white horse, Jason. The road to the wishing well was long and arduous. Normally he would have enjoyed the loveliness of the scenery, but now it depressed him. Black flowers had no charm and the blue woods were ghostly and chill. He was tired; he had ridden hard for many hours, and his horse was weary too. They must stop and rest at the next village. As they entered the market square, a cheer went up. 'Make way for our Prince! Prince Rupert, he has come to help us!'

The people crowded round him, all talking at once. Neighbours argued as to who was the first to notice the green sky and the blue grass. Many claimed to have seen Wacky Witch following a huge, dark cloud.

'Can you help us, sire?' begged a group of farmers. 'Our sheep were so upset when the grass turned blue, they fled away to the high hills. If we only knew their whereabouts! We need to get them back for shearing.'

Prince Rupert was sad; how could he help? These farmers were so confident in his wisdom. He ate his sandwiches in silence. There, that was better! Soon he must be on his way. He pulled out his kerchief to wipe his hands and felt the leather pouch with its three gems. Just what use were they?

He turned from the crowd and busied himself with Jason's harness. Deftly he removed the emerald – green as the grass should be. He gazed into its clear depths and saw the hills and valleys of his dear land. He moved it this way and that, entranced with the changing scene.

'My friends!' he shouted. 'Look into this glass of mine. See if you can find your sheep!'

The farmers jostled with one another to hold the wondrous emerald.

'Why there they are!' shouted one. 'We must hurry after them! What a marvellous glass this is!'

The Prince was happy he had solved one problem at least. Before he went, he arranged to have the emerald set up in a glass case in the market place, so it would be of use to all farmers for evermore.

Jubilantly he continued on his way, but he hadn't gone very far before he noticed the blue grass growing turquoise. Then pale green, then its own wonderful shade of green, once more. What a long way it was to the wishing well! Still, the scenery wasn't as unpleasant now, though horrid black flowers grew along the grass and the sky was a vivid green.

His horse neighed and threw back his head. Something unusual must lie ahead. They were approaching a cluster of cottages and the Prince could see people running around excitedly. A cloud of smoke billowed from the thatched roof of the middle cottage. Quickly Prince Rupert jumped from his horse and tethered him a fair distance away.

'Where is your nearest well?' he shouted. 'Bring pitchers and buckets. Hurry!'

It was a slow process drawing the water, but the Prince organised a chain of people to pass the water up to the cottages. Gallantly they all worked, but the roofs were damaged beyond repair. Someone prepared refreshments for the weary workers and they all sat by the wayside counting the cost of the disaster. Some cottagers had lost furniture and clothing in the fire; little children had lost toys. But – no-one was hurt. What a blessing!

Prince Rupert fingered his beautiful sapphire. Slowly he removed it from the pouch. 'This will pay for all the restoration. With the money left over, I will start a fund for others in a similar plight.'

The cottagers were overwhelmed with this generosity and would have had him stay, but the Prince was mindful of his mission.

Surely the wishing well couldn't be far off! He patted Jason and they galloped on their way; the Prince still thinking about the cottagers, and the way he would set up the fund. So bemused was he, he failed to notice the sky was slowly turning to its lovely blue. In the heart of a deep forest they found the wishing well. Rupert gazed into its green depths and, taking his remaining gem, the diamond, he dropped it in rather reluctantly. Now, all his jewels were gone! It was dusk and he barely noticed the green and golden goddess as she glided to his side.

'What can I do for you, Prince?' she asked.

'Oh, Green Goddess, our land has been struck by a wicked spell. Our flowers are black and so we cannot sell them or even enjoy them. Even the sky is . . . .' Here he broke off . . . . 'Why it is no longer green! It is the violet-blue of dusk!'

The Green Goddess smiled. 'That is your doing, Prince Rupert, not mine. Your emerald brought green to the trees and grass once more! Your diamond gift will beautify the flowers. Rest awhile in my forest home.'

She led him to a leafy bower and had no need to entertain him for he slept the sleep of exhaustion.

The following day Prince Rupert and Jason set out on their return journey. How successful the mission had been! See, all the flowers were pink and yellow, blue and mauve. What a marvellous picture they made! The Green Goddess had promised Rupert a gift; what could it be? When he came in sight of the city, his eyes were caught by a dazzle of light. White flowers were appearing in the hedgerows. How beautiful they were! He stopped to look; their centres shone like diamonds! Oh, he must take some to show his Princess! But he could not pluck one of them. The golden stems stood fast in the ground.

So, a rare and lasting beauty came to Flowerland and, because of them, Wacky Witch's spells no longer worked.

THE ENCHANTED FOREST

Some day, on your travels, you may be lucky enough to come across the Enchanted Castle. There you may join the other eager tourists and listen to the guide telling the magical story of long ago, but first you would need to walk along the stone jetty and sail across, for the castle is set like a jewel in the deep blue lake.

Lora and her two brothers, Shaun and Stefan, lived in a cottage in the heart of a vast forest of pine and birch trees. Their parents were dead and so Lora was mistress of the house and tended their every need. It was quite a happy existence. The brothers cut logs for the fire and Lora cooked and cleaned. Sometimes Shaun and Stefan would help out at the farm, outside the forest, and bring eggs, milk and butter in return. They were also adept at 'potting' a rabbit and Lora picked wild blackberries for pies and jam.

Occasionally they would muse about the Enchanted Tree which was said to be somewhere in the forest. Some folk said such talk was 'rubbish'. Others that the tree only became enchanted every thousand years. Rumours abounded about its special properties, but the fact remained, no-one had found the right tree. Well, was anyone surprised? There were thousands of trees in the forest. The boys and

Lora would amuse themselves dancing round a tree
chanting this ditty:

> *O little tree, O little tree,*
> *Shall we now your glory see?*
> *As around we sing and dance,*
> *Dress with gold your every branch.*

As time passed and nothing happened, they grew
tired, and very rarely indulged in the game. One day,
a lovely summer's day, the three were having a picnic.
The day was warm; no logs were needed for the fire.
The larder was full of freshly-baked pies, so Lora
quickly packed a basket and off they went.

'Where to this time?' enquired Shaun. 'Oh, let's go
to the edge of the forest, near the ravine. I love to see
the view far away over to the hills.'

It took quite a time to reach the edge of the forest,
but eventually, as trees thinned out, they came to a
dell, and sank down gratefully on the springy grass.
Lazily they passed the summer afternoon and only
exerted themselves sufficiently to enjoy their picnic
meal.

Lora looked around. 'Shall we play the tree game?
We haven't done for ages.'

The brothers groaned. 'She never gives up, does
she? Now which one is it today, Lora?'

She looked around, doubtfully. The trees might
have thinned out a little, but there were still so many
to choose from. 'Never mind, I'm going to the edge to
sit and admire the view.' She never tired of the vista.
For a long time she gazed with half-shut eyes at the
expanse before her.

'Come on,' she shouted to the brothers, 'time to be
off!'

Slowly she rose. 'What a funny little tree this is, not like the others at all. It's quite stunted. Come Shaun, Stefan, let us honour this little one and see if it grows in stature!'

Anxious to placate her and then to hurry home, the brothers joined hands and chanted their little song. 'Now, will you come home,' demanded Stefan.

Lora sighed; the little tree looked exactly the same –just a small fir tree, too small even for Christmas decorations. She hastened after her brothers, pausing to retrieve the picnic basket. How bright the sun appeared; a golden glow spread behind her! She suddenly caught her breath. Could it be, had they found the magical tree at last? She dropped the basket and dashed madly back to the edge of the forest. What a wonderful sight! The little tree decked in cloth of gold shimmering and sparkling from tip to toe! She clapped her hands together and knelt in the springy grass. The brothers found her so and joined with Lora in silent admiration. Something dazzled near the top of the tree. It was a beautiful mirror, its handle encrusted with pearls. With eager hands she clasped it to her and shyly took a look at her reflection. How surprised she was to see a pretty face! Lora hadn't time to wonder about her looks, she had a vague idea of her features when she gazed into the lily-pool. Nor did the brothers wish to encourage vanity in their sister.

Stefan was reaching up for a flute – a lovely golden instrument hanging by a golden thread. He put it to his lips experimentally; he had always longed for some such musical instrument. He would ask the Old Man of the Forest to teach him how to play.

Shaun was already tossing a beautiful golden ball. High in the air he threw it, exulting in the glory of its

118

spinning. So busy were they with their new possessions, they didn't see the gradual dimming of the tree and suddenly, like a light going out, the fir tree stood, ordinary and dark. But the gifts were real. 'Thank you little tree,' they cried, and hurried home with the treasures.

Stefan couldn't wait to try out his flute, and, later the following day, he set out to find the Old Man of the Forest who was only too delighted to give him lessons and to hear the wonderful story. In return, Stefan did odd jobs about his cottage.

Shaun never tired of playing and kicking the ball – not too far – he didn't want to lose it!

Lora sneaked frequent looks at herself in her mirror, so much so, that she sometimes let a pot boil dry or forgot a pie in the oven!

This went on for a few weeks. Shaun grew lazy – he was always amusing himself with the ball and neglecting to cut logs for the coming winter days. Lora was getting vain. She was no longer content just to busy herself around the house. She now had high ideas about herself. 'With *my* looks I should have someone to wait on me!'

Stefan was the only one who was content. He was making excellent progress and soon would be able to earn a good living in the town, playing his flute.

One awful day Lora burned her fruit pies. It would mean a long search of the bushes for more blackberries and, as she looked again in the pantry, she realised stocks were getting low. The brothers had not been helping out on the farm and she had been lazy and had not made jam or wine. Shaun was bad-tempered; he had spent all morning just kicking the ball about and he was ready for his dinner, but it was all burned! Lora and he had a terrible row whilst

119

Stefan was away visiting the Old Man of the Forest.

'We never rowed like this before,' sobbed Lora.

'No, that's true,' agreed Shaun.

'It's all the fault of the little fir tree!'

Shaun slowly shook his head. 'No, it is we who are at fault – we made bad use of its gifts.' So they made a solemn vow to put away their treasures. Lora hid the ball and Shaun hid the mirror.

Life went on happily for them. Lora cooked and baked and Shaun mended the roof and chopped wood. Stefan was now only a visitor – he was a good flautist and loved his busy life in town. Winter came and spring, then summer and, a year to the day, Shaun and Lora decided on another picnic.

'Shall we give our gifts back to the tree?' whispered Lora. 'Would it accept them? We have learned our lesson, but we shouldn't keep such treasures.'

Shaun agreed, and they brought the ball and mirror from their hiding-places.

Carefully they wrapped them and placed the mirror and the ball, along with the sandwiches and cakes, in the picnic basket. After their meal in the lovely dell, they made their way to the very edge of the forest and gazed silently at the little fir tree. Solemnly they circled saying:

O little tree, little tree,
Back we give these gifts to thee.
As we round you chant and dance;
Give to someone else the chance.

Nothing happened. Nothing at all. Uncertainly they placed the mirror and the ball at the foot of the tree. The journey home dragged. Now they had left the gifts they wondered if, after all, it had been a wise decision.

The following morning they were awakened by a loud knocking on the door. There was Stefan, sparkling with excitement. 'Come with me. Hurry, don't stop for breakfast. I thought I would make you a surprise visit but, on my way, what a surprise for me!'

Willy-nilly he tugged them through the trees till, breathless, they arrived at the edge of the forest.

'Oh, have the gifts gilded the little tree again?' asked Lora gasping. Then she stopped, in amazement. Down below stretched a long blue lake and, in the centre, was a fairy-tale castle, its turrets crowned with gold.

'Do you think . . . ?' Lora began. Then she knelt on the grass and put her arms about the little fir tree.

And there they lived in contentment, the castle doors only opening to the sound of Stefan's golden flute.

THE MAGIC BALLOON

Nancy had been to the fair. What a splendid time she had spent there, bobbing up and down on the horses to the jingle of the fair organ! She loved the gaudy colours of the painted stalls, decked with all manner of toys and knick-knacks to tempt little girls and boys. Fluffy monkeys and singing-birds on sticks vied with gaily-coloured balloons – round, sausage-shape and squiggly, in self colours or rainbow hues. A lovely smell of roasted potatoes pervaded the fairground and Nancy decided to spend a few more of her precious pence on a paper bag filled with the hot, salty treat. Anxiously she peered into her little red purse. Oh, dear! She had only enough money left for some toffee, or another try at the coconut shy – or a gorgeous big balloon.

She tugged at her father's arm. 'Do you think I could win a coconut, Daddy, or shall I buy a balloon?'

He smiled. 'I tell you what I'll do. I'll make certain of a coconut by buying one to take home to Mother, and you can have your balloon.'

Nancy clapped her hands with glee. 'Oh, thank you, Daddy, let's go right away to the balloon lady.'

She had already made up her mind which balloon

was her favourite – the lovely round one, white with rainbow markings. Carefully she counted out her money and took hold tightly of the string.

'Let's get out of this crowd quickly,' said Father, 'or else your balloon will soon pop or float away.'

All the way back home Nancy followed with rapt attention every sway of her gorgeous balloon. She even took it to bed with her and tied it to the bedpost.

The following day was nice and sunny, just right for playing out-of-doors, so, after her breakfast, Nancy untied her balloon and out she danced into the back garden. One or two little birds sat on the fence and gazed in amazement at the happy child with her big balloon. I think they thought she had somehow got the full moon on a string! The balloon was bobbing about in a mischievous manner. A slight breeze had got up and Nancy had to hold on more tightly to the string.

'Good gracious me!' she exclaimed. 'How rough it's getting.'

Her little legs began to run down the path as she was pulled along by the balloon. Faster and faster she ran, still gamely hanging on. The balloon seemed to have a mind of its own as if it knew precisely where it was going *and* was in a hurry too.

'Stop, stop!' cried Nancy. 'You're going much too fast!'

'Not at all,' squeaked a voice somewhere above her head, 'we'll never get to Balloon Land if we dilly-dally!'

'Dear me,' muttered Nancy. 'I do believe my balloon is talking.'

'Of course I am,' chuckled the balloon, 'and please call me Moony. We're nearly ready for take-off, hold tight!'

Nancy hadn't time to be frightened; up and up they soared. Why, she could see the fair down below! She really must have bought a magic balloon. Now they were flying so high that all the cows and horses looked like toy ones out of her wooden farmyard. A fluffy, white cloud was near enough to touch. Good gracious, they were going right into it! Soft as velvet it was, and deliciously warm. It was lined with another cloud, but this one was rosy-pink and, as they sailed up to it, Nancy could see it looked far more substantial.

'Not much further, my dear,' squeaked Moony. 'Here we come to the inspection gates. You don't have any pins or needles on you, do you?' he demanded anxiously.

'Of course not,' said Nancy indignantly. 'Mummy always mends my clothes properly and my hair is kept tidy with this blue Alice-band.'

'Good, good,' he beamed, 'here we are at the gatehouse. Don't let go of me till we are through the gates.'

A very majestic red balloon was on duty. 'Aha, whom have we here? Ah yes, it is down in the book that you are due for a short visit, Moony. I suppose you couldn't get here on your own, so you brought a visitor.'

'Well,' mumbled Moony, 'last night was my last chance, but she tied me to the bedpost!'

Here Nancy gave him an apologetic, yet slightly pleased, glance!

'But she's such a lovely child I thought I would give her a treat.'

'And a very nice thought too,' boomed Sunny, for that was the guard's name. 'Have a good time! I believe you have no pins, needles or clips to declare?'

126

'Indeed not,' they both chorused. Gaily the two bounced through the gates and down a winding path. Nancy could see a deep valley and, as they rounded the final bend there was the most magical sight she had ever seen.

Balloons of every description were gliding and sailing about. Some were at rest on the pink velvet. There were little ones and big ones, sausage-shaped ones and squiggly shapes. Red ones, red and yellow, green or blue, green and blue and oh, every imaginable colour and shape.

'Hi there Moony,' squeaked Dashy the sausage-shape. 'Who's your friend?'

'Why it's Nancy. We met at the fair yesterday. She chose *me* from simply hundreds of others,' boasted Moony, grandly.

'And quite rightly too,' murmured Dashy. 'Would she enjoy a little trip with me to the far corner of the valley?'

'Dear me no, thank you all the same,' said Moony importantly, 'we're going to visit the workers in the "pop" workshop.'

With a 'Hold on to my string again, Nancy', over they glided to a dome-shaped pink velvet 'cushion'.

'Here we are, this is where patches are invisibly fastened. One tiny hole can be so dangerous for a balloon.'

Inside were rows and rows of shelves containing pieces of every imaginable colour and pattern of balloon. Several balloon-men were hard at work, patching up holes on some worried-looking balloons.

'After a little rest they'll all be as good as new,' boasted Moony.

'What kind of thread or glue is it?' queried Nancy.

127

'Oh, that's very special, the Fairy Moonbeams spin it for us and it's rubbed very gently round the patch. The join never shows. Let us go to the Air Restorer now.'

On they floated to the far side of the valley where the air seemed so much fresher.

'Here we are, Nancy.' Moony alighted at the entrance to a tunnel. What a wind! Nancy had to hold on to her skirts as they moved down the corridor, lit by pretty pink stars. Inside a circular room lots of tired-looking and wrinkled balloons were awaiting treatment. The helpers were lady balloons and all were rainbow types.

'Yes, these are my relatives, Nancy. They do a grand job restoring these poor things.'

The ladies were so pleased to see the little visitor and offered her a gust of their revitalising air!

'Bye, now,' interrupted Moony, 'we must return before long. Our special cloud is drifting away from your home, Nancy. Soon it will take till tomorrow to get back. Your mother would be very worried.'

The little girl emerged from the tunnel feeling very refreshed. 'Let me say goodbye to your friends, first,' she asked. 'Maybe I'll see you sometime at the fair,' she added wistfully.

'Sure to,' grinned Dashy.

All too soon Moony and his mistress were gliding up the path to the gatehouse.

'Had a lovely time?' asked Sunny.

'Absolutely wonderful,' smiled Nancy.

'Come and see us again before long,' he boomed. 'Safe journey back!'

'Hold tight,' squeaked Moony, and off they flew down and down, till they could see once more the fields and the fair and, at last, Nancy's own back garden.

With a whoosh and a sigh she found herself sitting on the grass, the string still tightly clasped in her hand. The balloon was resting on the grass; there was no wind at all.

'I expect you're very tired after all that flying, aren't you, Moony?' she said, sympathetically.

But, do you know? He spoke not a word.

MAGIC BY THE LILY POOL

Long ago there lived a young lady whose name was Peta. She had four beautiful elder sisters and, unlike the Cinderella sisters, they were quite kind to their younger sister. You could call Peta the ugly duckling of the family; like her sisters she had lovely, golden hair and blue eyes, but her nose was large and irregular. Most people forgot all about it, for Peta was sweet of disposition, but extremely shy when in the company of young men and her sisters' suitors. She would avert her face and mumble her words so that usually the young men gave up and sought elsewhere.

Over the years first one, then another of her sisters married – all to very eligible partners. Peta's mother would sigh, 'Goodness knows when Peta will meet a nice young man. She's so shy and difficult in their company!'

Peta loved to roam in the woods surrounding their farm and she would also delight in visiting old Grannie Apple-cheeks. She would set off in the early morning, taking some special chocolate cakes which Grannie loved above anything else. They would spend the afternoon chatting over tea and Grannie would tell tales of long ago. Some people said she was a witch, but a kindly witch. Peta didn't care – she always looked forward to her visits.

131

On this particular visit, a warm day in early June, they were sitting out of doors sipping Grannie's home-made lemonade. Peta was not her usual bright and cheery self, Grannie Apple-cheeks could see that. 'A penny for your thoughts, Peta,' she smiled.

The girl was silent. Then she said, ruefully, 'Did you know my eldest sister, Mary, is to have a baby at Christmas?'

'Oh, how delightful,' crowed the old lady, 'now I shall be able to use the soft white wool I have by me and make some bootees. But you look so solemn, Peta, won't you be thrilled to be an auntie?'

'Of course! But do you think *I* shall ever be married, Grannie, and have a family?'

'No doubt at all,' clucked Grannie Apple-cheeks sharply. 'It won't be long before a handsome man whisks you away!'

'With *my* looks?' mourned Peta sadly.

'No-one notices your big nose except you yourself, my girl, but you frighten everyone away with your sullen responses!'

Nevertheless the old lady was worried. Peta was a favourite of hers; time was passing. She herself would dearly love to see the girl happily married before she died.

'Run along and gather some of my favourite flowers from the woods. I have something to look up in my Special Book.'

Peta wandered through the dells, gathering blooms of white and blue for Grannie Apple-cheeks to arrange in her lovely pewter vases. When she returned the old lady was sitting in her rocking-chair, looking very satisfied with herself.

'Come and sit down Peta. I'll arrange the flowers later. I have something to say to you. Will you be able

to visit me on Midsummer's Day?'

'Why, yes, I think so.'

'Yes, but can you arrive very early in the morning?'

'I suppose that can be arranged.'

Peta was intrigued. Gone was the wistful look from her face. 'Why, Grannie?'

'Just you wait and see!'

On the way home Peta thought about nothing else but Grannie's forthcoming surprise. Gaily she completed her tasks – milking the cows, feeding the chickens, tending her own garden and the hundred and one things needed to be done by her on the farm. Midsummer's Day seemed a long way off, though it was only 17 days. Carefully she crossed them off her calendar. Her mother and father were quite happy for Peta to visit Grannie Apple-cheeks for the day, but were a bit anxious about so early a start. No-one would be about. So they insisted that Sport, the labrador, should accompany their daughter.

Bright and early she awoke and tiptoed downstairs to eat a quick breakfast of porridge and coffee. Sport roamed up and down the big, blue and white kitchen. He sensed a carefree day with his beloved mistress –a holiday in fact! Softly they went out of the door and made their way through the misty woods. Not a soul did they encounter – not even the birds were about – but Grannie Apple-cheeks was up!

'Come on in, my loves – I have a special Midsummer's Day surprise for you. Just for today, you know. I want you to go to the Lily Pool, the beautiful green water covered with water-lilies. Cover your face with the water, then take out a mirror I shall give you. One thing you must remember, don't look into the mirror until you've dipped your face in the pool.'

Peta was mystified. She couldn't understand why she needed a mirror. Surely she could find a spot in the pool clear enough to see her reflection! However, Grannie was always right. How exciting today was!

'Mind you,' called the old lady, 'it's only magic for today! Hurry now, you must be there before the mist clears.'

Sport and Peta hurried along. It wasn't far to the pool. How dark it looked! The water was still and green and covered with big, creamy-white water-lilies. She knelt down on the bank. Ugh! Some of this seemed a mite weedy. Peta preferred to wash her face in rainwater – it kept her face smooth and soft.

Sport gazed in surprise as his mistress dipped her face in the green murk. No accounting for taste! Peta wiped the surplus off and couldn't wait to take out the dainty silver mirror from its pouch. She peered intently. What a nuisance the mist was still about, but ah! Suddenly the sun peeped out and she stared with surprise as she gazed at the pretty face in the mirror. Certainly her nose had shrunk – it was quite a different shape too! Oh, how marvellous! Sport licked her face; his mistress puzzled him this morning.

'Come on, let's stop all this nonsense and have a game or two!' Peta hugged him and skipped merrily round and round. Then a thought came over her; Grannie had promised magic for just today. She must make the most of it. So this was how it felt to be beautiful!

The sun was warm and comforting as Peta, tired at last, sank onto the grass with Sport at her side. She looked dreamily at the pool and smiled. The lilies reminded her of breakfast cups set on green trays! On she dreamed, but then she dreamed she had lost her mirror and she awoke with a start.

135

Sport was tugging at her dress. A few yards away stood a young man smiling down at her. With a flourish he removed his green feathered cap. 'I'm sorry if I startled you – may I sit awhile and share with you this lovely Midsummer's Day?'

Peta was confused, then remembered she had no need to turn her head away. 'Of course, come and share with me the sandwiches Grannie Apple-cheeks has made.'

She chattered on, happy in the knowledge of her attractiveness. Intently he listened, enchanted with her conversation and wit. So the hours passed till, reluctantly, Peta realised she must make her way back to the cottage. Grannie would be worrying.

'Come again,' he implored. 'Let's meet here in a month's time!'

Peta paused. In a month's time things would be quite different. Beauty would be no longer hers. 'I'll see,' she cried, rushing off through the trees, Sport at her side. Only then did she realise she knew nothing at all about this young man. She had been so busy chattering on about her own affairs!

Breathless, she reached the cottage. 'Grannie,' she called. 'It worked, it really worked. I *am* beautiful today. See!'

Grannie Apple-cheeks smiled at the radiant face. 'Did you meet anyone by the pool, Peta?'

'Why, yes, a fine young man.'

The old lady chuckled delightedly. 'He comes every Midsummer's Day from a land far off. You see, some years ago, he was riding in the forest, when suddenly his beloved horse, Jess, bolted. He was thrown, but the poor horse fell from the boulders by the waterfall and was killed. She's buried by the pool.'

'Oh, poor young man, he never told me!'

136

'Perhaps he never told you he is a prince, eh?'

Peta's eyes popped with astonishment. Then, sadly she said, 'He wants to meet me again by the pool – in a month's time, but I can't go. He thinks I'm beautiful.'

Grannie Apple-cheeks looked a bit bothered, then decided to prepare some tea. A nice cup of tea always refreshed a body and put a cheerful slant on things! They munched the little chocolate cakes in silence, then briskly the old lady spoke.

'Peta, I have something to confess. Will you forgive me for being a crafty old lady?'

The girl was amazed; what was there to forgive? Today had been simply marvellous. Nothing could take away her memories of such a magical time!

'You see, Peta, the special mirror I gave you is magic. Look in it tomorrow or any day; you'll always look beautiful!'

Peta was puzzled. What was the problem?

Grannie began to look a bit guilty. 'Peta, my love, we all think of you as a lovely young woman. You have enchanting ways – we never notice your nose – really we don't. Today you met a stranger – I planned it so. The mirror made it possible for you to be your own sweet self; it gave you confidence. The prince was enthralled with you.'

'So,' whispered Peta very slowly, 'I wasn't beautiful at all.'

She fingered her nose. Yes, it felt as big as ever! What a fool she had been! She looked at Grannie reproachfully. 'How could you, how could you?'

Peta dashed off through the woods, reliving the events of the day. She wasn't seeing the prince again! Not likely! How forward she had been! How confident in her charm! Her family couldn't learn

137

much from Peta during the following weeks. Certainly she did all her tasks in a right and proper fashion. Every now and again, she was heard to mutter, 'No, definitely *no!*' Then sometimes, 'We-ell, perhaps I could just peep!'

In the end the decision was taken from her. Apparently Grannie Apple-cheeks was a little under-the-weather. Peta was to take a bottle of medicine along with the chocolate cakes. Apparently her appetite was still in good order!

Slowly Sport and Peta set off through the woods to see the old lady.

'Ah,' said she, 'how nice to see you, and with my favourite cakes too. I just need some flowers to brighten my bedroom.'

A coy look came into her eyes. 'The purple ones, near the Lily Pool, they would look just right in this pink vase!'

Peta looked at her suspiciously, but the invalid was leaning back on her pillow. Nothing for it but to creep through the trees; the prince would get tired of waiting. She could bide her time. But, of course she had reckoned without Sport. Really, he was a most disobedient dog today. One sight of the prince and he dashed to him, licking him all over.

Peta hid behind her tree; nothing would induce her to come out. The prince rose to his feet and then she noticed – he was limping. All her motherly instincts were aroused. She dashed forward and watched happily as his face lit up with pleasure. Such a lot of explaining had to be done then in the rest of that golden afternoon.

Of course they were married, but first Peta asked of her prince, 'Tell me, John, what did you first notice about me?'

He smiled understandingly. 'Why, your wonderful expression my dear!'

And so, Peta was content.